MOUNTAIN JACK PIKE

HARD FOR JUSTICE

#8

MOUNTAIN JACK PIKE

HARD FOR JUSTICE

#8

Robert J. Randisi

SPEAKING VOLUMES, LLC
NAPLES, FLORIDA
2013

Hard for Justice #8

ISBN 978-1-61232-599-6

PROLOGUE

Pike knew that the man was inside the big tent that served as a whorehouse for the settlement of Clark's Fork. Ted Clark, who owned the trading post and was unofficial booshway of the settlement, was a good friend of Pike's, but the big mountain man had not even told Clark that he was in town. He had arrived shortly before dark and had secreted himself, waiting for darkness to fall. During that time he had spotted his prey, walking across the settlement, and entering the whorehouse tent.

Skins McConnell was supposed to meet Pike at Clark's Fork the next morning, and he had urged Pike not to do anything until he got there. Pike had greeted that request with silence, which McConnell might have taken for assent. More likely McConnell knew that Jack Pike would do whatever he damn well pleased.

Now that it was good and dark, with only a sliver of a moon to light the way, Pike made his way to the big tent and entered.

The madam, who had seen Pike there many times before, knew who he was, although she had never called him by name, and likewise he had never called her by name – hell, he didn't even *know* her name.

As she approached to greet him, Pike held his finger to his lips. She frowned, and frowned even deeper when she saw the Kentucky pistol in his hand.

"What is it – " she said in a low voice, but he waved her off.

"A man came in shortly before dark," Pike said, whispering. "A tall, slender man with a scar across his right cheek and big jug ears. Do you remember him?"

"Yes, I remember him," she said. "Is he a friend of yours?"

"I'm going to kill him."

"Not in here!" she said, urgently.

"Then I'll take him outside," Pike said. "Who is he with?"

"Colette."

Pike frowned. When he was in Clark's Fork, he often stopped to see Colette. The blonde whore was popular. That was because she liked her job, and she liked it even better with certain men, one of whom was Pike. But that was before Pike had settled in with Sun Rising. The big mountain man hadn't gone a-whoring since.

"All right," Pike said, taking the woman's elbow, "call Colette out."

"What do I tell her?"

"I don't care, "Pike said, squeezing her arm, harder than he'd intended, hurting her.

She led him along the blanketed cubicles that passed for rooms in this makeshift whorehouse. When they reached Colette's cubicle they stopped.

The madam gave Pike a quick frightened look, and pushed aside the blanket.

"Colette, I need you," Pike heard her say.

"Hey, what's this—" a man's voice complained, but then Pike heard Colette's soothing voice.

"Easy, honey," she said, "I'll be right back, don't worry. You won't go anywhere while I'm gone, will you, lover?"

"I'm not going anywhere, girlie," he said. "Just get back here soon, huh? It was just starting to get interesting."

"Colette!" the madam said.

"All right!"

The madam backed out and Colette appeared, totally naked, as beautiful as Pike remembered, even though he hadn't seen her in six months.

Colette noticed Pike right away, but before she could say his name he pressed his hand over her mouth.

6

"Stand back," he whispered.

She did as she was told. Pike, holding his Kentucky pistol in his right hand, pushed aside the blanket and stepped into the cubicle.

"Back already, darlin? —" the man on the bed said. But his voice died when he looked up and saw Pike standing there.

"What the —"

"Another word and I'll kill you right now, "Pike said.

The man frowned, but remained silent. He was completely nude and, until moments ago, he'd had an erection.

"Get dressed."

Pike cocked the pistol. Slowly the man got up off the bed and pulled on his pants. He was reaching for his shirt when Pike stopped him.

"That's enough," Pike said. "The pants are enough."

"It's cold outside, friend!"

Pike stepped forward and pressed the barrel of the pistol against the man's nose.

"I ain't your friend!"

"All right, all right," the man said, "I'm sorry. Jeez, Mister, what the hell —"

"Let's go."

"Where?"

"Outside."

"Can't you tell me —"

Pike backhanded the man across the face. It was a powerful blow that brought blood to his nose.

"Shit!"

"Outside!"

Pike saw the man's eyes dart to the side and knew what he was looking at. As soon as Pike had entered the cubicle he'd located the man's weapon, a pistol like his own. The man was measuring the distance between himself and the weapon and trying to figure his chances.

"The odds are very bad, Mister," Pike said, "but be my guest and try it."

The man only glared at Pike, trying to staunch the flow of

7

blood from his nose with his hand.

"Smart choice," Pike said. "Now let's go outside."

Pike marched the man out of the cubicle and to the front entrance of the tent. Outside the temperature was below freezing, and there was snow on the ground.

"Out!"

"Jeez, Mister—"

"Out!" Pike snapped, and gave the man a powerful shove that sent him sprawling onto the ground.

"Don't move," Pike said.

"Can't I stand up?"

"Not yet."

Pike waited a few seconds until his night vision adjusted and then said, "Stand up."

"Jesus, Mi-mister," the man said, standing up, "I'm freezing."

"You won't be cold for long," Pike said. "What's your name?"

"Haywood."

"Where are your friends, Haywood?"

"W-what friends?"

"Four men," Pike said. "You and four men raped and killed a Crow squaw two weeks ago, and burned down her house. I want to know where the others are."

"Jesus, I don't know," Haywood said. "We split up—"

"You're not giving me the answer I want, Haywood, so might as well kill you now."

Pike pointed the pistol at the man's head. "Wait, wait, Jesus," he cried and ducked, covering his head with his arms.

"What am I waiting for?" Pike asked coldly.

"Let me think."

"Think fast," Pike said. "Give me some names."

"Names?"

"Of the men you were with."

"Okay, okay," Haywood said, "wait—Jeez, I'm so cold I can't think. My feet are frozen!"

"If I shoot them off they won't be cold," Pike said. "Come on, names!"

8

"All right, all right," Haywood said, "there was Hecox, uh, Murphy, and — and Raitt a-and . . . Tilson!"

"Hecox, Murphy, Raitt and Tilson. Have I got them right?"

"Yeah, yeah, that's them."

Pike already had the descriptions of the men; now he had the names to go with them — if the man wasn't lying.

"Drop your pants," he said to Haywood.

"What?"

"I said drop your pants!"

"W-why? I told you —"

"You could be lying," Pike said. "I'm going to ask you again with my knife against your balls. If I think you're lying, I'm gonna cut them off."

"Jesus . . . no! I ain't lyin', Mister, I swear!"

"Drop your pants."

"I can't!" Haywood said. "Please, Mister —" He dropped to his knees in front of Pike. "Please!"

"Did she plead, too?" Pike asked. "The Crow woman? Did she plead with you?"

"Come on, Mister," Haywood said, "she was just an Indian. Why are you doin' this? She was just a squaw."

"To you she was just a squaw," Pike said, "to me she was *my* squaw. Open your mouth."

"W-what?"

"Open your mouth, damn it!"

Haywood stared at Pike, then slowly opened his mouth. Pike inserted the barrel of his pistol into the man's mouth, and Haywood's eyes went wide with fear.

"Hecox, Murphy, Raitt and Tilson," Pike said. "Have I got that right?"

"Yuh," the man said, nodding his head vigorously. With the barrel of the pistol in his mouth he forgot all about the cold.

"You're not lying?"

Tears rolled down Haywood's face as he shook his head to indicate he wasn't lying.

"That's good," Pike said, "that's real good. Now, tell me

9

where I can find them."

Haywood started to babble and Pike was able to make out just enough of it to understand that the man was claiming — he didn't know where any of the others were.

"I'll tell you what, Haywood," Pike said. "I'm going to make it easy on you. Just tell me where I can find one of them."

Haywood closed his eyes and started weeping uncontrollably.

"One name, Haywood," Pike said, prodding the barrel of his gun against the back of Haywood's throat until the man gagged. "One simple name. All right?"

Haywood opened his eyes, looked up at Pike and nodded his head. Pike withdrew the barrel from his mouth, but kept the muzzle right in his face.

"Hecox," Haywood said.

"Where?"

"H-he said he was going to a Snake village, somewhere near the Y-yellowstone."

"Why there?"

"He spent a long time with the Snake Indians," Haywood said, talking fast. "Might even have grew up with them. I don't know. C-come on, man! I gave you what you want, didn't I?"

"Yes, you did," Pike said, "and I thank you."

Haywood started to say something, but he never got a chance to finish. Pike pulled the trigger of his pistol. A hole appeared in the man's face as the lead ball crashed through his lips and teeth and blew out the back of his head. Blood and brains and tissue splattered the snow.

As the man fell Pike stuck his pistol back into his belt. When he turned around he saw the madam and Colette — wrapped in a robe, now — staring at him in horror.

"I hope he paid in advance," Pike said, and walked away.

PART ONE

VIOLATION

CHAPTER ONE

Two weeks earlier

Jack Pike met Skins McConnell at the agreed upon place on the Green River. He could tell from the glum look on his friend's face that he'd had no better luck than himself.

"Traps empty?" Pike asked.

McConnell lifted his arms in a helpless gesture.

"Traps empty," Skins said.

They'd set beaver traps up and down the river, and along the tributaries, and not one trap had yielded a beaver.

"Sit down and have some coffee," Pike said, lifting the pot from the fire. McConnell grabbed a cup and held it out for Pike to fill. When he tasted the brew he made a face.

"Your coffee's gotten worse since Sun Rising started living with you," McConnell said.

"Well, thankfully, I don't have to drink my own coffee very often."

"How long's it been, Pike?" McConnell asked. "Five months."

"More like six."

"I can't hardly believe it."

"What? That she's been with me for six months?"

"No," McConnell said, "that you ain't had another woman but her in six months."

"What makes you think I haven't?"

McConnell stopped with his cup halfway to his mouth and peered at his friend from beneath his hat.

"You mean you have?"

13

"I didn't say that."

"Well, you ain't sayin' you have, and you ain't sayin you haven't."

"That's right."

"Is that any way to treat a friend?"

"A nosy friend, yeah," Pike said, grinning.

"Ah," McConnell said, "whether you have or haven't, I still can't hardly believe that you've kept her this long."

"I haven't kept her," Pike said. "She's free to go anytime."

"Yeah, not much chance of that, is there?" McConnell said. "She still looks at you the same way she looked at you the first time we saw her, remember?"

"I remember."

"She took a shine to you right off."

Truth be told, McConnell had taken a shine to Sun Rising right off, but the Crow woman had eyes only for Pike. Pike had resisted her until they were thrown together during a bear hunt with an infamous Russian hunter. They had been through a lot together, and had been together ever since.

It surprised the hell out of Pike. He'd never been a man to stick to one woman before. He'd had many women over the years, and had left many women behind.

Sun Rising had been the first he'd taken with him.

"I guess the beaver are really gone," McConnell said, forlornly.

Pike appreciated his changing the subject, but the subject his friend had chosen was a particularly sad one. For the last few years, beaver had become more and more scarce, and now it looked as if they were gone, altogether.

"Maybe we should start hunting bear," Pike said.

"Are you kidding? After what we went through the last two times we went after a bear?"

"Yeah," Pike said, "yeah, I guess you're right." He dumped out the remainder of his coffee and then emptied the pot. "Well, we might as well get back to the cabin."

14

Allan Hecox reined his horse in with one hand and tilted up a bottle of whiskey with the other.

"Don't drink that all yourself," Mitch Murphy called out. He rode up on Hecox quickly and snatched the bottle away, sloshing some of the liquor onto his horse's neck.

"Don't spill it!" Dan Tilson shouted.

Bert Raitt and Jake Haywood brought up the rear and watched their partners fight over the bottle, which ended up on the ground.

"Shit!" Tilson shouted.

Raitt, the unofficial leader of the pack, urged his horse on and rode past the bickering men. Jake Haywood, a born follower, did just that.

Raitt was forty, tall and broad-shouldered. He was the kind of man who needed to have men follow him; that was why he took to Jake Haywood from the moment they met. Haywood was tall as Raitt, but some fifty pounds lighter, and while Raitt was ruggedly good-looking, Haywood was a homely man with big, jug-handle ears.

"They're all drunk," Haywood said.

"I know," Raitt nodded. "Maybe one of them will fall off his horse and kill himself. Is that a cabin?"

"Where?" Haywood asked, looking around.

Raitt saw that Haywood was looking in the opposite direction. He reached over and slapped the man in the back of the head, knocking his hat off.

"Over there, stupid. Through those trees!"

Haywood turned back and peered through the trees.

"Yeah, yeah, it's a cabin, and there's smoke coming from the chimney."

"Collect those three morons and follow me," Raitt said. "I want to check it out."

"Sure, Bert."

Raitt gave his horse a kick and started forward. Only somebody who didn't want to be found would build a cabin way up here where nobody ever came. Raitt and his men wouldn't be here either except they had just robbed a settlement and killed three people – a man and two women – and they didn't want to run into anyone for a while, either.

As Raitt approached the house, he could hear the others riding up behind him. He felt a tingle of excitement, because he didn't know what they were going to find inside.

When Sun Rising first heard the horses she thought it was Pike and McConnell. She started for the door, and then stopped when she realized that there were more than two riders approaching.

She walked to the fireplace and took down the rifle hanging on the wall above the mantel.

As they dismounted Hecox asked, "What are we doing here, Raitt?"

"We need a place to hole up."

"So? Somebody lives here."

"Sure," Raitt said, "they live here *now.*"

"Stupid," Murphy said to Hecox.

"Who you calling stupid?" Hecox demanded.

"That's enough, you two," Raitt said. "Hecox, take Tilson and go around back. Don't come in until I call you. Understand?"

"Sure, I understand." Hecox cast a murderous look Murphy's way and added, "I ain't stupid."

After Hecox and Tilson had gone around back Raitt approached the door with Haywood and Murphy.

"We just gonna go in?" Murphy asked.

"Somebody livin' out here all alone hears a bunch of riders, what do you think they're gonna do?" Raitt asked.

"I don't know."

Raitt looked at Haywood and shook his head.

"They're gonna be on the other side of this door with a rifle," Raitt said. "Murphy, go over by the window and when I give you the signal throw something through it."

16

"What?"

"I don't care what," Raitt said, "just throw it when I give the word."

"Okay," Murphy said. He started toward the window, then turned and asked, "What's the word?"

Raitt closed his eyes and wondered why he didn't have at least one man he could talk to.

"I'll wave my hand," he said patiently, "like this."

"Wave your hand," Murphy said. "I got it."

"Good."

Raitt stood to one side of the door and Haywood the other.

"After he breaks the window," Raitt said to Haywood, "you go in. Right?"

"Right," Haywood said, never questioning why he should be the first one through the door.

Raitt looked at Murphy and waved his hand. Murphy, instead of picking something up and getting ready, waited until that moment to look around for something to throw. Disgusted, Raitt waited until Murphy finally pulled the knife from his belt and waved back. Raitt waved harder, and Murphy threw the knife through the window.

The glass crashed and a shot was fired. Meanwhile Haywood hit the door with his shoulder. It crashed open and he rushed in, followed by Raitt.

Raitt saw the Crow squaw aiming the rifle at the window, and quickly crossed to her and snatched the gun from her hands.

"Well, well," he said, looking her up and down with pleasure. "Ain't she pretty?"

"Sure is," Haywood said.

"Can I come in now?" Murphy asked, sticking his head in the door.

"Yeah," Raitt said, "and get those other two morons, too."

"Right."

"Look around," Raitt told Haywood.

17

There wasn't much to look at. The cabin had only one room, and there was obviously no one else present. There were, however, indications that someone else lived there.

"Where's your man?" Raitt asked.

Sun Rising did not answer.

"Squaw, I asked you a question," Raitt said. "Where's your man?"

Still she didn't answer, and Raitt slapped her full across the face with the flat of his hand. As he did his breathing quickened. The trickle of blood that formed at the corner of the squaw's mouth was like a red flag to a bull.

He wanted her.

As the others entered the room Raitt said, "Spread her out on the floor, guys."

"All right!" Haywood said, knowing what was going to come next.

He and Murphy grabbed the woman and dragged her to the floor. They each held one of her arms, while Hecox and Tilson held her legs. She was wearing a buckskin dress, and as Raitt straddled her, he tore it from her body. Her full, brown-tipped breasts bobbed into view and Raitt, who was fitting to bust his britches, stood up and dropped his pants. His hard, but not very large erection lay flat against his stomach.

"When I'm finished with you, squaw," he said, leaning over her and running his cock over her belly, "my friends are going to take their turns, and then I might take another . . . and then I'll ask you again where your man is."

Sun Rising spat in the man's face.

He laughed coldly and savagely grabbed her right breast, making her cry out.

"That's just gonna make it better."

When they were finished, Raitt sent the others outside. He sat on the floor next to Sun Rising, who stared up at the ceiling, as she had been doing for the past hour, while the men grunted and rutted above her, emptying themselves into her, sinking their teeth into her soft brown flesh. She had bloody bite marks on her shoulders, neck, and breasts, and one of the men had cruelly bitten through her bottom lip, which was now swollen to twice its normal size.

"Whoowhee!" Hecox shouted outside. "That sure was one sweet tastin' woman."

Raitt listened as the other men laughed and agreed.

"Now, sweetheart," Raitt said, settling his hand onto Sun Rising's belly. She twisted, trying to shy from his touch, but he grabbed the tight flesh of her belly and slowly slid his hand down, sinking three fingers inside of her.

"Where is your man?"

Sun Rising turned her head, looked at him, and again spit in his face.

"Bitch!" Raitt hissed. He pulled the pistol from his belt, pressed the barrel against the side of her head, and pulled the trigger.

CHAPTER TWO

"Another hour and we'll be there," McConnell said, as they stopped to rest the horses. "I can taste Sun Rising's cooking now."

"Oh, you don't mind her being around when she cooks, huh?"

"I didn't say I mind her bein' around," McConnell said. "Hell, that's your business, Pike."

"But you don't think she'll be around much longer, do you?"

"Whataya mean?"

"I know what you're thinking, Skins. I know you real well, remember."

"All right," McConnell said, relenting, "all right, no, I don't think she'll be around much longer."

"You think she's gonna leave? Or do you figure I am?"

"You are," McConnell said. "Remember, my friend, I know you real well, too. You ain't never stayed with one woman this long."

"And what's that tell you?"

"That you're ready to bust out."

"Well," Pike said, "maybe you're wrong. Maybe I ain't ready to bust out. Maybe I never will be ready."

"You gonna marry her?"

"Can't say," Pike said. "I can't say right now, but that's a possibility."

"Never."

"We'll just have to wait and see, won't we?"

"I guess so."

* * *

Raitt came out of the cabin, reloaded his pistol, and tucked it back into his belt.

"Go inside," he told the others, "take whatever we can use, and then burn it."

"Burn it?" Murphy asked.

"Burn the house down, stupid," Hecox said.

"Who're you callin' stupid?" Murphy demanded as he followed Hecox into the house.

As Haywood started after them, Raitt put his hand on his arm to stop him.

"Take Tilson and have a look around. We still don't know where her man is."

"If we find him?"

"Kill him."

"And if we don't find him?"

"Then he'll find her when he gets back," Raitt said, "won't he?"

"Smoke," McConnell said. "She must know we're coming. She's cooking."

"She's always cooking," Pike said, frowning. "But that's too much smoke, Skins." McConnell could see the alarm on his friend's face.

"Too damn much smoke," Pike added, and gave his horse his heels. McConnell was right behind him.

Pike had built the cabin here, among the trees, so that it would be hard to see. Somebody would have to come upon it by accident. That was why they didn't see the blazing cabin until they were only twenty yards away.

"Oh, my God," McConnell said.

The cabin was not yet completely ablaze, which meant that the fire hadn't been burning for long.

Pike dismounted on the run and rushed to the front door

21

of the cabin.

"Pike!" McConnell shouted. He didn't want his friend rushing headlong into a fire, but there was nothing he could do to stop him.

There was a stream nearby, but there was no chance they could carry enough water from it in time to save the cabin.

They could save Sun Rising, though, if she were still inside.

McConnell dismounted and ran to the front door. As he reached it Pike came staggering out, holding Sun Rising in his arms. The way her head was hanging, McConnell knew she was dead.

"Is there anything else—" McConnell started, but he stopped. He was going to ask Pike if there was anything else of value in the cabin, but that was just plain stupid. He followed Pike as he carried Sun Rising a safe distance from the house and put her down on the ground.

"Pike—"

"She's dead, Skins," Pike said. He was kneeling over her, his hands hovering above her body, as if he didn't know where to put them. "Look at her, she's naked, she's been shot . . . what the hell happened here?"

Skins stared at the dead woman and saw the bite marks on her body. It wasn't hard to figure what had happened. She'd been raped, and then shot, and then the cabin set afire . . . but why?

"Jesus—" Pike said, finally putting one hand on her forehead. "Jesus . . ."

McConnell stood up and looked at the cabin. It was now totally ablaze. He looked down at the ground, then walked away from Pike, to give his friend some time alone.

He walked around the cabin, studying the tracks in the soft ground, and pretty soon he had it figured.

When he returned to Pike, his friend had regained his composure, but looking into his eyes, McConnell could see the anger simmering just beneath the surface.

"What did you find?" Pike asked.

"Four or five riders, probably no more than an hour ahead of us."

"We can run them down."

"How? We don't know who they are."

"Five men riding together? How many groups of five men do you think we'll find around here?"

"Pike, she has to be buried."

Pike looked down at Sun Rising, then back at McConnell.

"Skins, you bury her."

"What?"

"Bury her for me, will you . . . please? I've got to get started."

"Pike — "

"Skins, I'm asking you — "

"All right, all right," McConnell said, cutting him off. "I'll bury her, but you've got to promise me something."

"What?"

"Meet me at Clark's Fork in two days? All right?"

Pike didn't answer.

"All right, Pike?"

"Yeah, all right, Skins."

"Clark's Fork," McConnell said, "two days. You can't track all five of these men alone."

"If I have to," Pike said, "I will."

"Don't worry, Pike," McConnell said, "you won't have to."

McConnell watched Pike ride away and knew in his heart that his friend should have taken some time to grieve before setting out on his hunt. As it was he was a mountain ready to explode. McConnell wished he could have gone with him, but Sun Rising had to be buried.

McConnell walked to his mule and pulled down a shovel.

23

When she was properly buried, he stood by her grave, wondering what words he should be saying. He was still wondering when he saw a blur of movement in the trees. He stared hard, and saw it again.

There was somebody there.

"Hey!" he shouted. "Hey, you!"

Whoever it was started running, and McConnell took off after him.

His quarry zigzagged through the trees, so it was difficult to make out who it was. When McConnell thought he'd gauged which way the other runner was going, he switched direction, hoping he was guessing right.

He did.

As their paths crossed, McConnell dove, catching his quarry around his narrow hips. He pulled him down to the ground and rolled him over.

It was a boy, an Indian boy of about twelve.

"Take it easy," McConnell said, "I'm not gonna hurt you."

"I am not afraid of you," the boy said defiantly.

"Well, that's good," McConnell said. "I'm gonna let you up. But if you run again, I am going to shoot you in the leg. Understand?"

The boy just glared at him, but he could see that he understood. He rolled off the boy and hauled him to his feet.

"What were you doing back there?"

"I was working."

"For who?"

"For Sun Rising," he said. "I – I ran away from my village, and – and I was lost and I was hungry. She told me that she would feed me, but that I must work for my food."

"Did you see what happened?"

The boy looked away. "Is she dead?" he asked in a low voice.

"Yes."

"She was nice."

24

"Yes, she was."

"Did you see what happened?"

Now the boy looked straight at him.

"Yes."

"Did you see who did it?"

"Yes."

McConnell's heart began to race.

"Would you know them again if you saw them?"

"I would know them," the boy said, "I would know them all."

McConnell put his hand on the boy's shoulder and said, "Come with me."

He truly wished now that Pike hadn't run off the way he did. They had a witness, and with a witness it would be a lot easier to find the guilty men.

What he really feared was that Pike was so angry he might end up killing the first man who crossed his path . . . guilty or innocent.

He knew if that happened, Pike could never live with himself.

CHAPTER THREE

Two weeks later

Ted Clark stared across the table at his friend Jack Pike, wondering what to say next.

"Jack," he said, finally, "you just plain blew the man's head off . . . while he was on his knees! If we was anywhere near a lawman, you'd be in jail right now for murder."

"It wasn't murder," Pike said, "it was justice. I told you—"

"Yeah, I know," Clark said. "You told me about what they did to Sun Rising."

"How would you feel if it was Sky Woman?" Pike asked, referring to Clark's Crow wife.

"I'd feel the same way you do," Clark said, "but what if you had killed an innocent man?"

"He wasn't innocent: The two women heard him say he was in on it. They heard him give me the names of the others."

"I know," Clark said, "they back your story all the way. But what I'm sayin' is—"

"Look, Ted," Pike said, "unless you plan to lock me up someplace, I need to get some rest. Skins will be here tomorrow, and we'll start after the other men."

"Do you know where they are?"

"I have an idea where one of them is," Pike said. "Haywood told me before . . . he died."

"There's something I don't understand."

"What's that?"

"How did you know Haywood was headed here?"

"I didn't," Pike said, "but I knew one of them was. They'd split up about a day's ride from here, and I had to pick one track to follow."

"How did you know this man Haywood had a scar?"

"I ran into a couple of hunters along the way and they described him to me."

"A man with a scar," Clark said. "Could have been a hundred men. You had no way of knowing he was the one—"

"Are we going to go through that again? He was one of them, and that's that. Now he's dead, and I can go on to the next one."

As Pike stood up Clark said, "Pike, all I'm sayin' is next time try to be more careful before you kill a man. You might kill the wrong one."

"Don't worry," Pike said. "I'll be killing the right ones."

"Where are you gonna stay tonight? I got a bed out back—"

"Don't worry about it," Pike said. "I'll be staying with Colette."

Clark stared questioningly at Pike. Sun Rising was only dead two days and already Pike was going to stay with a whore?

"I need a place to stay, and I need be with someone," Pike said simply.

There was also the fact that Colette said she wouldn't back his story if he didn't come and stay with her, but he didn't tell Clark that.

"I'm not such an evil woman," Colette had said to him. "You need to be with someone, Pike, and I want to be that someone. Is that so bad?"

He'd told her that as long as she backed his story, he'd come back, and she had, so he owed it to her.

Clark watched Pike leave his trading post and decided he'd have a talk with McConnell when *he* arrived tomorrow. Hopefully, Pike would wait for his friend and not move out at first light.

Clark had never seen Jack Pike so angry and frankly it scared him.

The Crow boy's name was Little Fawn, and he hated it.

"What's wrong with it?" McConnell asked.

"It is not a warrior's name."

"You'll get your warrior's name when you get older."

"It is a girl's name, not a boy's."

"Why did your mother name you that?"

"She says when I was born I had the eyes of a fawn," the boy said, with disgust.

Little Fawn was riding behind McConnell as they rode for Clark's Fork. McConnell hoped that Pike would keep his word and wait for him. It was important that Little Fawn describe the men to Pike, this way Pike would know exactly who he was going after.

When they camped the first night McConnell had cooked up some bacon and beans. The boy ate with a voracious appetite.

"You keep eating like that and you'll be as big as a warrior before you know it."

The boy looked up and smiled, and then bent his head back to his plate.

During the second day of travel the subject of names

came up again.

"I do not want you to call me Little Fawn."

"Then what do you want to be called?"

"I do not know."

"Well, let's see. Maybe we can come up with a name for you, huh?"

They rode in silence for a while, thinking it over.

"I know," McConnell said, "why don't we just call you Buck."

"Buck?"

"Well, it's something we whites sometimes call an Indian, a buck."

"What does it mean?"

"Well, when I use it I mean . . . a young warrior. Some people mean something else."

"Buck," the boy said. "Yes, I will be Buck."

And from that moment on, Buck was his name.

Pike returned to the whore tent that night and found Colette waiting for him.

"Come on," she said, "you need some sleep."

"How does your boss feel about this?"

"If she doesn't like it, she loses her best girl," Colette said. "Don't worry, no one will bother us."

She led him to her blanketed cubicle and sat him down on the bed. She removed his boots, put aside his weapons, helped him with his pants. Pike didn't realize how tired he was until she slipped off his shirt and laid him down.

She blew out the lamp, then dropped her robe, and crawled into bed next to him. She was naked, and her flesh was burning hot. Pike's body reacted quite naturally. She pressed her breasts against his back and draped one arm over his hip. Her hand lay precariously close to his erection.

"Did you love her, Pike?" she whispered.

After a moment he said, "I don't know."

"The way you shot that man," she said, "the anger in you—"

"It doesn't matter whether I loved her or not," he said. "They shouldn't have killed her, they shouldn't have . . . done the things to her that they done."

She felt him growing angry again and kissed the back of his neck.

"Shh," she said, "let's not talk about it. Go to sleep."

In the morning Pike awoke and, for a moment, did not know where he was.

He felt a woman pressed against him and knew it wasn't Sun Rising. He took a moment to collect himself and survey his surroundings, and then he remembered where he was.

He also discovered something else. He still had a full erection, and sometime during the night Colette had closed her hand around it.

He rolled onto his back, and she moved in her sleep to accommodate him, but she didn't release her hold. He wondered what time it was, and decided to get up.

He tried to slide away from Colette without waking her, but her hand would not let go.

"Colette," he said, gently.

Her head was on his shoulder, her fragrant blond hair draped across his chest. Suddenly, she opened her eyes and looked at him.

"Pike . . ." she said, sliding her hand up and down his shaft.

Pike was only human, and she was a beautiful, sweet-smelling woman. He slid one hand over her hip, down between her thighs, and slid one finger along her slit, which instantly grew moist. She lifted her leg over him, climbed onto him, and took him inside of her in one swift motion that made her gasp.

As she moved over him, riding him, she began to breathe heavily. Pike lay still, allowing her to use him, but unable to deny the pleasure she was bringing him. He cupped her buttocks in his big hands and she fell onto him, her breasts mashed against his chest. As they moved together, her breath came quicker and then she suddenly tensed and shuddered. Pike exploded into her with a groan, and then held her tightly in his arms.

"I'm sorry," she whispered in his ear.

"Don't be," he said. "I'm much too big for you to have forced."

She laughed softly and rolled off him.

"When will you leave?"

"Today," he said, "soon. What time is it?"

She rolled over and looked at a time-piece he could not see.

"It's eight o'clock."

"I don't expect Skins until sometime near eleven. If he's not here by noon, I'll leave."

"Why didn't he come with you?"

He sat up in bed and swung his feet to the floor so that his broad back was to her.

"He stayed behind . . . to bury Sun Rising."

Suddenly, she felt guilty, and figured that he must be feeling it, too.

"Can I get you some coffee?" she asked.

"Sure."

She slid out of bed and put on her robe. "I'll be right back," she said.

She left him and he continued to sit there, naked, thinking about the events of the night before. He re-

31

membered vividly the look on Haywood's face just before he pulled the trigger. He didn't regret doing it, and he wouldn't regret killing the others.

He might regret it later, but he didn't allow himself to think about that now. Sun Rising deserved to be avenged, and he would deal with the consequences of exacting that revenge later.

Much later.

CHAPTER FOUR

Well before noon Skins McConnell rode into Clark's Fork with the Indian boy he called Buck riding behind him. He directed his mount to Ted Clark's Trading Post, where he and the boy dismounted.

They went inside and he found Ted Clark behind the trading post counter rather than behind the bar. It was a little early for bar business.

"Skins," Clark said, "am I glad to see you."

McConnell decided that meant trouble.

"Pike got here?"

"Last night," Clark said. "He killed a man, Skins. He had him on his knees and unarmed, and he blew the poor bastard's head off."

McConnell thought about that a moment, then said, "Well, having seen what they did to Sun Rising, I can't work up any sympathy for the bastard."

"But that's not like Pike—not the Pike we know."

"He isn't the Pike we know, Ted," McConnell said, "and he won't be until this is over."

At that point Sky Woman came out of the back room, and Buck saw her. They instantly recognized each other as Crow, and that seemed to make Buck nervous.

"Take it easy, Buck," McConnell said, feeling the boy tense. "This is my friend Ted Clark, and his wife, Sky Woman."

"Where did you get the boy?"

"He was there, Ted," McConnell said. "He saw what the men did to Sun Rising."

"You poor boy," Sky Woman said. McConnell could count on the fingers of one hand the times he had heard Sky Woman speak.

"How about letting Sky Woman get the boy some food?" Clark said. "And you, too."

"I have to find Pike, but let the boy eat," McConnell said. "Buck, go with Sky Woman. She'll fix you something to eat."

"You will come back?"

"I'll be back."

"You will not leave me here?"

McConnell put his hand on the boy's shoulder.

"I said I'd be back, don't worry. Now go ahead."

Reluctantly, Buck allowed Sky Woman to steer him to the back room.

"What was the boy doing there?" Ted Clark asked.

"He ran away from his village, and Sun Rising was feeding him. She sent him for wood, and when he returned he saw the men. He was afraid, so he stayed outside and watched. When he heard them laughing he got curious. He sneaked closer to the house, looked in the window, and saw them raping her."

"Damn!"

"Ted," McConnell said, "they savaged her like animals. They took turns with her, and then shot her in the head."

"Jesus," Clark said, "no wonder Pike's so angry. I mean, if they had just killed her . . . but to abuse her like that . . ."

"And then burn down the cabin."

Ted Clark shook his head in wonderment that there were such people in the world.

34

"Where's Pike? Where did he spend the night?"

"He's with Colette."

"Colette? The whore?" McConnell asked in surprise.

"I don't think he wanted to spend the night alone."

"I'll go and tell him I'm here."

"If I know Pike, he's gonna want to leave right away. I'll outfit you."

"Thanks. I'll settle up when I come back."

"No settling up to do, Skins," Clark said. "I'm doin' this for Pike."

"Thanks, Ted."

"You gonna take the boy with you?"

"I don't know," McConnell said. "He saw the men responsible. He can identify them."

"Sky Woman would like it if you left him here."

"Yeah, but I don't think Buck would like it too much."

"Buck?"

"That's what we agreed we'd call him, until he got his warrior name."

"And what's his real name?"

McConnell shook his head "That's a secret between Buck and me."

Clark laughed, "It must be some name."

"You'd think so, were it yours," McConnell said on his way out.

McConnell had almost reached the tent when he saw Pike come out. The big man squinted at the brightness of the sun, and then looked down at the snow. From where he stood, McConnell could see that the snow had a pinkish tinge to it. Pike looked up and spotted Skins.

"What the hell were you doing in there?" McConnell asked. It came out much harsher than he had intended, but then he'd been the one left behind to bury Sun

Rising while Pike was out here a-whorin' with Colette.

Pike frowned at his friend, unaware what he had done to offend him.

"Skins—"

"Forget it," McConnell said quickly. Maybe Clark was right. Maybe Pike simply hadn't wanted to spend the night alone. Who could blame him? He had just killed a man, and that never sits easy.

"You want something to eat?" McConnell asked.

"Sure," Pike said, "but then we've got to get moving. I've got a line on one of the other men."

"What about the others?"

"Three more, after that. There were five altogether. When we find the second one, he'll tell us where the others are."

"What if he doesn't know, Pike?"

"He'll know," Pike said. "Those kinds of snakes always know where to find one another."

"Pike—"

"Are we gonna eat?"

"Yeah," McConnell said, "yeah, we're gonna eat."

Pike looked behind him at the tent, then at the pink spot in the snow, and then at McConnell.

"Let's go."

As they approached the trading post McConnell said, "Look, there's something I got to tell you."

"Can you tell me inside?"

"I'd rather tell you before we go inside."

Pike stopped with one foot on the bottom step and said, "So talk."

McConnell had never seen Pike look so cold, so unemotional.

"How do you feel?"

"I feel fine," Pike said. "Is that what you wanted to talk to me about?"

"No," McConnell said, "no, I want to talk to you about Buck."

"Who's Buck?"

McConnell told Pike about the Crow boy he'd found at the cabin.

"And he saw everything?"

"That's right."

"And can identify the men?"

"He says he can."

"How old is this boy?"

"About twelve."

"And you believe him?"

McConnell thought a moment, then said, "I don't have any reason not to, Pike."

Pike looked up at the door to the trading post, and then back at his friend.

"Where is he now?"

"Inside," McConnell said, "Sky Woman is giving him something to eat."

"Let's ask him if one of the men had a scar."

"The man you killed had a scar?"

"That's right."

McConnell thought a moment.

"Well, we could have the kid look at the man and see if he was one of them."

"No, Skins," Pike said, "he was one of them. I don't need the kid to tell me that. Besides, there isn't much to look at. I just want to know if he says that one of them had a scar on his face, because then I'll know he really saw what happened."

"And then what?"

"And then maybe we'll take him with us," Pike said.

"So he can point them out, and you can kill them?"

"That's right."

"You'd do that to a little boy?"

"Let's go in and ask him," Pike said, "before we argue about it."

"All right," McConnell said, "let's ask him."

When they walked inside, the boy, Buck, was sitting at one of Ted Clark's homemade tables. Ted had made them all out of empty barrels.

"Food?" Clark asked.

"Yeah," McConnell said, but he was looking at Buck.

Pike walked over and stood opposite the boy, who stopped eating to stare up at him. He had never seen a man so big.

"You speak English?" Pike asked.

"Yes."

"Keep eating," Pike said.

The boy obeyed, but kept staring up at Pike.

"My friend says you saw who killed Sun Rising."

"Yes."

"Who did it?"

"Five men."

"Will you know them again when you see them?"

"Yes."

"All of them."

"Yes."

"Was there anything special about any of them?"

"Yes."

The boy's answers came without hesitation. Pike liked that about him.

"What?"

"One of them had a very big nose."

"And?"

"One had very big ears."

"Anything else?"

"One was very big," Buck said, then added, "but not as big as you."

"What else?"

Now Buck hesitated, his fork halfway to his mouth.

"Anything else?"

"No," Buck said.

Pike stared at the boy a few moments, then turned and walked back to McConnell.

"He didn't see anything," Pike said. "He's just after some free meals."

"Pike—"

"Let's eat over here."

"Wait."

They both looked over at Buck, who was standing up now.

"What?" Pike asked.

"One man," Buck said, "had a scar, right here." He ran his hand along his right cheek to illustrate.

McConnell looked expectantly at Pike, who was staring at the boy.

"Sit down and eat, son," he said finally. "You're gonna need all your strength for the trip."

The boy sat down and continued to eat.

Pike turned and saw McConnell staring at him.

"I won't argue about this," Pike said, quickly, urgently. "He can identify them, and I need him."

"He's just a—"

"Ain't you the one who was worried about me killing an innocent man?"

McConnell just stared.

"Well, he'll keep me from doing that, won't he?"

No answer.

"Won't he?"

"Yeah," McConnell said, "sure, he'll keep you from doing that."

"Let's get something to eat, and get outfitted."

"Ted's takin' care of that," McConnell said, sitting down.

"Well then, I'll pay him."

"He ain't chargin' us."

"Oh," Pike said, sitting opposite him.

Sky Woman came out with two plates of food and set them down. Pike watched her turn and walk away, and then he fell to eating. He ate without tasting, ate only to sustain himself for the killing ahead.

In half an hour, the three of them would be on their way. There were still four men to catch, and kill, and he had an appetite for only one thing: revenge!

CHAPTER FIVE

Allan Hecox hated Indians. He also hated the fact that he had grown up with Indians—specifically, the Snake Indians.

He had been born in the mountains, and when his parents were killed during a raid he had been raised by a Snake squaw. While growing up, the Snake children made fun of him, and the young braves shunned him. His Snake mother, however, the squaw Walking Fawn, always welcomed him into her camp. She extended to him her protection, which was considerable, considering her present husband was the famous Black Cherry Joe.

In contrast to Hecox, Black Cherry Joe, although a full-blooded Snake, had lived many of his formative years among the whites. Because of the dark color of his skin, the whites had named him Black Cherry, meaning to mock him. Instead, he rose to power among the Snake Indians, and kept the name the whites had given him.

So when Allan Hecox rode into the Snake camp, Black Cherry Joe allowed him to stay to please Walking Fawn. Although Walking Fawn was ten years older than Black Cherry Joe, he valued her as his wife. She was a good cook, a strong worker, and she satisfied him at night, when they shared his blankets.

For all of this, he put up with her "son," even though Black Cherry Joe knew that Hecox hated Indians. The only time he ever came to camp was when he was in trouble.

"How long will he stay this time?" Black Cherry Joe asked Walking Fawn.

"I do not know," she said. "Not long, I think."

"What is he running from now?"

Walking Fawn looked at the floor of the teepee and said, "I do not know."

Black Cherry Joe grunted. Whatever Hecox was hiding from he was too cowardly to face alone. The Snake leader knew that Hecox traveled with a pack, and it was only when he was with the others that he showed any courage at all.

"Are you cooking for him?" Black Cherry Joe asked his wife as she bent over the fire.

"For him," she said, "and for you."

Her husband grunted again, and left the tent.

Walking Fawn knew that her son was a coward, and that he only came to her when he was in trouble, but she had raised him and she loved him. She also loved him because he was the only child she would ever have. She had never been able to have babies of her own. That, she knew, was another reason that Black Cherry Joe had taken her as his wife.

The Snake leader did not want any children, and did not have to worry about her becoming pregnant.

She continued to prepare dinner for her two men, hoping that while Allan was in camp, she would be able to keep him and her husband apart.

Hecox hated coming back to the Snake camp. If Raitt hadn't ordered him to hide out, he never would have returned. He didn't think much of Walking Fawn, and very little of the Snake Indians in general. The Crow, now there was a people who knew how to deal with their enemies. The Blackfoot, also. Black Cherry Joe was too soft, and he made the Snake Indians as soft as he was.

When Hecox left the tribe as a young man, he had taken back his white name, Allan Hecox. He never thought about the name Walking Fawn had given him, anymore. He had never spoken the name or thought of it since the day he left. He had never told the others — Raitt, or Tilson or the rest — his Indian name.

He moved to the flap of the tent and peered out. He chose to stay inside to avoid as much as possible any contact with the Indians — unless there was a squaw he wanted. The women never refused him, because they looked on him as Black Cherry Joe's son, even though the Snake leader was only about ten years older than Hecox.

That was the only good thing about coming back. He could have any woman he wanted, married or not. That was what he meant about being soft. The husbands never challenged him because of Black Cherry Joe. If this were a Crow or Blackfoot camp, it wouldn't matter who his father was. If he went after another man's wife, the husband would kill him in an instant.

He looked outside again, waiting for Walking Fawn to come with the food. As he did, he saw a young Snake girl. She couldn't have been more than sixteen. She had lustrous black hair, and her breasts were like little buds beneath her buckskin dress. Her legs were strong looking, with high calves and nicely turned ankles.

He would arrange with Walking Fawn to have the girl brought to him later. Right now what he wanted was some goddamn food!

Pike and McConnell had spent a hard winter on the Yellowstone River a couple of years back. Winter was almost gone now, and it wasn't nearly as cold as it had been back then.

They rode single file, Pike in the lead, Buck between them, and McConnell taking up the rear. If they ran into any Crow, they'd have to explain about the boy, but they were more likely to run into the Blackfoot, or the Snake—and it was the Snake they wanted.

When they made camp for the night, McConnell looked across the fire at his friend. Pike was speaking very little these days, and McConnell talked mostly with the boy. In fact, he and Buck had become fast friends during the week since they'd left Clark's Fork.

Now, however, McConnell spoke to Pike.

"You know, when we find the Snake Indians, they might be Black Cherry Joe's bunch."

44

"I know."

"How do you think he'll feel about this?"

"Joe hates all whites."

"Why would he be letting Hecox hide with them, then?"

"I don't know," Pike said. "I suppose we'll have to ask him, won't we?"

"I suppose so," McConnell said.

That was all he was able to draw out of Pike that evening, so he returned his attention to Buck, whose English was getting better and better.

The boy had learned English from some white missionaries who had lived with his people when he was smaller — until the Crow had tired of them and killed them. McConnell figured the boy must be smart as a whip to have retained it this long, and to be improving his command of the language so rapidly.

That evening McConnell decided to take the boy to the river to try and catch some fish for dinner. Pike stayed behind, frying up bacon and making the coffee. When McConnell and the boy returned with their catch — a huge catfish — they proceeded to cook it in the bacon grease.

After dinner, Pike took the first watch. McConnell bedded the boy down, then slid between his own blankets. From his vantage point, he could see Pike's face in the light from the fire. It was like stone. His friend hadn't been eating much during the week, and McConnell thought he could see the effects. Pike's cheekbones were more prominent, and when he stripped off his shirt to take his morning dip, there was no sign of the extra weight he'd been carrying around his waist for the past few months. Pike was down to fighting weight, for sure, and McConnell now realized that the weight loss had more than likely been deliberate. Pike was hunting five men — four, now — and was preparing himself for a long hunt by hardening his body.

If McConnell was going to stay with him, he knew he would have to do the same, but he was worried about the boy. He was going to have to convince Pike to let the boy go — but go where? Buck didn't want to go back to his own people. He wanted to grow up too fast, and by witnessing what had happened to Sun Rising, he had made a good start.

If McConnell allowed Pike to use the boy, Buck was going to grow up a lot faster, still.

When Walking Fawn brought Hecox his food, he grabbed the wooden bowl from her, sat on the floor, and began eating with his hands.

"How long will you stay this time?"

He looked up at her with grease smeared around his mouth.

"You want to put me out already?" he asked. "I just got here."

"No one wants to put you out, my son —"

"Oh no?" Hecox asked. "How about ol' Black Cherry Joe? I'll bet he was real glad to see me."

"Do not antagonize him, Allan," his mother warned. "Every time you come —"

"Every time I come he gives me a hard time. He hates me and you know it."

"Please," she said, not wanting to get in the middle of their fighting, again. She hated to admit it, but she too was sad when she saw her son.

"Are you in trouble —"

"You think I only come here when I'm in trouble?"

"You do not come to see me," she said, "and you do not miss our people so much that you—"

"They're *your* people," he snapped, "not mine."

"That is why I ask—"

"I'll be here a few days," Hecox said, "no more. I'll be out of your hair before you know it." He finished what was in his bowl and pushed it away, just short of throwing it at her. "How about some more? That is if your husband hasn't eaten the rest?"

"I will get you some more," she said, with a sigh.

He followed her to the tent flap. The young squaw he had seen earlier was still by the fire.

"Who is that?"

Walking Fawn saw the girl he was talking about, and her heart sank.

"Her name is Little Doe."

"She has a man?"

"Yes."

"Who is he?"

"Strong Bear."

"Strong Bear," Hecox said derisively, shaking his head. "I want her. Bring her to me later."

"Please, Allan—"

"Bring her to me!"

She stared at her son for a few moments, then said, "I will bring her."

She left and he let the flap fall closed.

After dark, Walking Fawn returned to Hecox's tee-pee. She entered, followed by Little Doe, holding her head low.

"Leave us," Hecox said.

"I want—"

"Leave us!"

She closed her mouth, nodded, and backed out. Hecox wondered what Black Cherry Joe had ever seen in her. No one had ever called Walking Fawn a pretty woman, even when she was young.

Hecox approached Little Doe, and slowly walked around her, looking her over. She was small, but her body was firm. He put his hand against the small of her back and felt her flinch.

"Do you know who I am?" he asked.

"Yes."

Her tone was very low.

"Who am I?"

"The son of a chief."

Well, he thought, that was close enough.

He sat back down on his blanket.

"Remove your clothes."

She hesitated, but did as she was told. When she was naked, he saw that he had been correct. Her breasts, though small, were round and firm. Her belly was flat, her hips wide, and her thighs muscular. She was just the kind of woman some young buck would want for a squaw.

He wondered if her man knew she was with him.

"Come to me," he said.

She hesitated again, then walked to him, and stopped in front of him. He ran his hand up one leg, and down the other, squeezing her thighs and calves as if she were a horse he wanted to buy. He slid his hand up her inner thigh and tugged on her black pubic hair. Smiling, he inserted one finger inside her. She was dry when he entered her, but she soon became moist. He removed his wet finger and, smiling at her, licked it while she watched.

"All right," he said, reaching for her, taking her by the waist, "let's get to it . . ."

CHAPTER SIX

Hecox was with the Indians three days when Pike, McConnell, and Buck ran into a Snake hunting party.

"Easy," Pike said as five Snake braves came into view ahead of them.

The Indians, spotting the two white men and the Indian boy, looked them over curiously.

"We must run," Buck said.

"No, Buck," McConnell said.

"But . . . they will kill us."

"Not necessarily," McConnell said.

"Then we will kill them?"

"No."

"I do not understand."

"Quiet," Pike said. "Both of you, be quiet." Then, as if as an afterthought, he said, "Boy, just watch, listen, and learn."

Buck looked at McConnell, who nodded.

Both parties waited and watched, and when Pike suddenly started his horse forward, the Indians moved, also.

Pike took the lead, with McConnell and Buck, riding just behind.

50

When there was about ten feet separating them they all stopped.

"I am Pike," Pike said.

"We know of Pike," one young warrior said. "He-Whose-Head-Touches-The-Sky."

"I am looking for a man who might be staying with your people."

The warrior did not respond.

"He is a white man."

"Why do you seek this man?"

"He raped and killed my woman," Pike said. "He and four others. I have killed one of them already."

"And you would kill this one?"

"This one, and the others."

The warrior seemed to be considering Pike's words.

"I am Strong Bear," the warrior said.

Pike didn't know the name, so he said nothing.

"The man you seek?" Strong Bear said. "His name is . . . He-cox?"

"That's the man."

Strong Bear stiffened and sat straight up on his horse.

"I will take you to him," Strong Bear said, "but you must promise me one thing."

"What's that?"

"You must promise to kill him."

Pike stared directly into the young warrior's eyes and said, "That is already a promise I have made to myself."

"Now you must promise me."

"All right," Pike said, "I promise."

Strong Bear stared at Pike a few moments

longer, as if gauging the value of his promise, and then nodded.

"We go."

Instead of following the five Snake braves, Pike, McConnell and Buck rode among them. Pike rode up front with Strong Bear.

"The boy is Crow," Strong Bear said.

"Yes."

"Why is he with you?"

"My wife was Crow," Pike said. "The boy saw who killed her. He will identify the men so I can kill them."

"I, too, wish to kill the man, He-cox."

"Why haven't you?"

"His mother is married to our chief."

"Black Cherry Joe?"

Strong Bear looked at Pike sideways and said, "Yes, that is his name. Do you know him?"

"I know him, and he knows me . . . but that doesn't mean that he'll be especially glad to see me."

"You come with me," Strong Bear said. "He will respect that."

Pike hoped that Strong Bear was right.

"There is something you should know about He-cox," Strong Bear said.

"The reason he stays with your people?"

Strong Bear nodded.

"His mother," the young warrior said, "is Black Cherry Joe's wife."

Along the way McConnell came up next to Pike.

"When we ride into the camp," Pike said, "Hecox won't know us." He went on to tell McConnell what Strong Bear had told him, that Hecox's mother was Black Cherry Joe's wife, and she was the only reason the Snake leader let him stay in camp.

"You can't just kill him outright," McConnell said. "Not if he's Black Cherry Joe's son . . . sort of."

"According to Strong Bear," Pike said, "Black Cherry Joe would just as soon kill Hecox as look at him."

"That don't mean he's gonna let *you* kill him," McConnell said. "He could have done that himself a long time ago."

"Well, I'll just have to convince him."

"And if he won't let you?"

"We'll just have to wait and see what happens," Pike said.

McConnell didn't say anything.

"Skins, you and the boy don't have to come into the camp," Pike said. "You can make camp yourselves, and wait for me."

"No," McConnell said, "we'll go along. I'd like to see what happens first-hand."

"What about the boy?" Pike said. "They might kill us."

"Even if they kill us," McConnell said, "they won't kill the boy. We'll go along."

When they rode into the Snake camp they were the center of attention. Someone must have run ahead and told Black Cherry Joe, because he was waiting in front of his teepee when they reached him.

Pike waited until Strong Bear and his men dismounted. Only then did he dismount, followed by McConnell and Buck.

Pike looked around at the people in the camp. He didn't see a single white man.

"Pike," Black Cherry Joe said.

"You remember."

"I remember."

The last time they saw each other it was about some white men who were stealing Snake Indian ponies. Pike and McConnell had to get them back to keep Black Cherry Joe and his tribe from taking their revenge on an entire settlement of whites.

Pike and Black Cherry Joe stared at each other across the camp. The Snake leader looked just as Pike remembered him. His skin was stretched so tightly over his cheekbones that it was seamless, hiding his age. He had long black hair, streaked with gray — perhaps more gray than the last time they'd met.

"I will speak first to Strong Bear, to see why he brought you here," Black Cherry Joe said finally, "and then I will speak with you, to see why you came here."

"All right," Pike said.

The older brave looked at the young one, and then turned and entered his teepee. Strong Bear followed, and Pike went over to stand with McConnell and Buck. Their horses had already been led away with the Indian ponies.

"Well," McConnell said, "we're here."

"Yes," Pike said.

"Are they going to kill us?" Buck asked.

McConnell looked down at the Crow boy.

"Are you afraid?"

"No," Buck said, and then nodded, "yes."

"Good," McConnell said, putting his hand on the boy's shoulder. "It's good when you can admit that you are scared."

"Are you scared?" Buck asked.

"No," McConnell said, then laughed and said, "Hell yes."

Buck smiled, "Good."

Pike surveyed the camp, looking for some sign of Hecox. He hoped that the man hadn't already left, or that one of the Snake braves hadn't already killed him.

Maybe the man was still in his teepee with Strong Bear's woman. Pike admired Strong Bear for admitting what had happened to Little Doe. The warrior had courage.

"Why don't you kill him yourself?" Pike had asked.

"He is under the protection of Black Cherry Joe," Strong Bear said, "or I would."

Pike wondered if, in the young warrior's place, he would have been able to exhibit such admirable restraint. He had no doubt that Strong Bear was not afraid of Black Cherry Joe; instead he respected his leader enough to suffer such an indignity.

So, he had forced from Pike a promise to do what Pike had intended to do, anyway.

Pike wondered if the young brave was explaining that to Black Cherry Joe at that very moment.

"So," Black Cherry Joe said, "you brought him to kill Hecox."

"I cannot kill him myself," Strong Bear said, "because I am loyal to you."

"Loyalty that shall be repaid."

"You cannot kill him, because of Walking Fawn. But this man has every reason to kill him," the young warrior went on, "and no reason not to."

"You are right," the older man said, "and I know Pike. He would snap Hecox like a twig . . . but I cannot allow it."

"Not in camp," Strong Bear said.

"That is right," Black Cherry Joe said, "not in camp."

"I understand," Strong Bear said, "but there is another way."

"What way?"

"Make them both leave."

"Walking Fawn does not want Hecox to leave—" Black Cherry Joe frowned. "To her, he is still her only son."

"But if he brings danger to our people," Strong Bear said, "you can send him from camp, can you not?"

"I could," Black Cherry Joe said, "but Walking Fawn would not—"

"You are the leader," the young man reminded him. "If you sent him from camp to protect your people, there would be nothing that she could do."

Black Cherry Joe made a painful face.

"She *could* stop cooking for me."

Strong Bear grinned and said, "But she would

not do that."

Black Cherry Joe did something then that very few men had ever seen him do . . . he smiled.

CHAPTER SEVEN

Strong Bear came out of Black Cherry Joe's tee-pee and walked up to Pike.

"Your friend and the boy will be taken to a tee-pee," he said. "There they will be fed, and wait for you."

"And me?"

"You are to go inside," Strong Bear said. "He will speak with you, now."

Pike nodded, and turned to McConnell.

"Go ahead," McConnell said, "we'll be fine."

Pike nodded, then ducked his head and entered the teepee.

There was a fire in the center of the teepee, and Black Cherry Joe was seated cross-legged on the ground on the far side. Pike had a feeling that they had been through all of this before.

"Sit."

Pike sat and waited.

"Strong Bear tells me you wish to kill this man Hecox," the Snake leader said.

"That's right."

"Tell me why."

Pike told Black Cherry Joe what Hecox, Haywood and the others had done to Sun Rising, and to their home.

"How do you know it was him?"

"Haywood, the first man, he told me—and he told me where to find him."

"But how can you be sure?"

"The Crow boy," Pike said. "He saw them. He will identify Hecox."

"I cannot allow you to kill him."

"I understand that he is your son-in-law."

Black Cherry Joe made a chopping gesture with his right hand.

"He is not my son-in-law," he said. "He is the son of my squaw."

"Not by blood."

"That does not matter to her," Black Cherry Joe said. "I feel your pain, Pike, but I cannot allow you to kill him. Not here, anyway."

"Explain."

"You could throw him out of camp."

"You and Strong Bear think alike," Black Cherry Joe said.

"I'll take that as a compliment," Pike said. "If Strong Bear made the same suggestion, what did you tell him?"

"I was tempted," Black Cherry Joe said, "but I cannot do that, either."

"You must think a lot of your wife."

Black Cherry Joe closed his eyes. "She is a good cook."

"I'm sure she is," Pike said.

He stood up and so did Black Cherry Joe.

"You are welcome to stay the night, but then you must leave."

"I understand."

59

Pike lifted the flap of the teepee and then he stopped and turned back.

"There is another way, Black Cherry Joe."

"What way is that?"

"If we let Hecox know why I'm here, will he fight, or will he run?"

Back Cherry Joe laughed.

"He will run," he said. "He is a coward, without a gang behind him."

"Are there any braves here who might stand with him?"

"Hecox hates Indians, and everyone here knows that. No, none of my braves will help him."

"Then he'll run," Pike said, "and I'll catch him and kill him away from camp."

Black Cherry Joe took a moment to think it over, then said, "If he finds out why you are here, I have no control over that, or what happens after he leaves."

"That's all I wanted to hear."

"You will not cause trouble in camp!" Black Cherry Joe warned him.

"No trouble in camp," Pike promised, and left.

Pike was shown to the teepee where McConnell and Buck were already eating.

"What is it?" Pike asked, pointing at the meat.

McConnell shrugged, a chunk of meat in his hand.

"Buck says he knows what it is, but I told him not to tell me."

"Fair enough," Pike said, taking a greasy chunk. "I won't ask either."

60

Buck laughed. The lower half of his face was covered with grease.

"What happened with Ol' Joe?" McConnell asked.

"He doesn't like Hecox any better than Strong Bear does, but he won't allow anything to happen to him while he's in camp."

"So what do we do now?" McConnell asked. "Wait until he leaves?"

"I won't touch him until he leaves," Pike said, nibbling at the meat, "but I don't want to wait until *he* decides to leave."

"Ah," McConnell said, "you want to force him out. How do you propose to do that?"

"All Hecox has to do is hear that I'm here looking for him," Pike said, "and he'll run."

"And you'll catch him."

Pike nodded. "And kill him."

"You want the boy to spread the word?"

"Kids talk to kids."

"And kids talk to parents. What do you say, boy?" McConnell asked.

"Will it help?" Buck asked.

"It will help," Pike said.

"Then I will do it," Buck said, and started to get up. Pike put his hand on the boy's shoulder to keep him from rising.

"You can do it after you eat."

Hecox was thinking about Little Doe. He'd enjoyed the young squaw, even though she hadn't contributed very much. She was inexperienced and he had more than enough time to teach her. He didn't have to meet Raitt and the others for a month, yet.

He decided to go for a walk, and let the people get a good look at him. It gave him a feeling of power, knowing that they didn't like him — even hated him — but that none of them would dare to make a move against him.

He strolled about the entire camp, watching the women as they did the laundry, and the old men as they made bows and arrows. The braves, those who weren't out hunting, gave him murderous looks, and he smiled back at them smugly. He passed a group of children who were playing, and they stopped to stare at him. He stared back, trying to frighten them, and then, bored, he went back to his teepee.

He didn't know if he could take a few weeks of this, but if Raitt ever found out that he didn't hide out, he'd probably kill him.

When Walking Fawn brought him his dinner that night he'd tell her to bring him Little Doe again. That should liven things up a bit.

Buck tried to mingle with the children, but they didn't want anything to do with him. He was standing around, watching them play, when a white man walked by. Buck stared at him, remembering his face, and as soon as the white man left, the boy went back to the teepee.

"He is one of them," Buck told Pike and Mc-Connell.

"You're sure of it?" McConnell asked.

"I am sure."

Pike leaned over and took hold of the boy's arm.

"Thank you, Buck."

The boy smiled.

"What do we do now?" McConnell asked. "Where did the man go?" he asked Buck.

"Back to his teepee."

McConnell looked at Pike.

"If he doesn't come out again, and if he doesn't talk to anyone, how will he hear that you're here looking for him?"

"There is one way," Pike said.

"How's that?" McConnell asked.

Pike stood up.

"I have to go and find Strong Bear," Pike said. "With his help we can get the word to Hecox with no problem."

"How?"

"I'll tell you after I've talked to him," Pike promised, and left . . .

Pike sought out Strong Bear and found him. The brave was talking to a young squaw of rare beauty outside of his teepee. They seemed to be arguing — actually, Strong Bear seemed to be pleading — and the girl was just shaking her head, looking sad. Pike waited until the squaw walked away, crying now, and then approached the warrior. When Strong Bear looked up he could see the anger in the young man's eyes.

"She is very beautiful."

"She will not listen," Strong Bear said.

"She is loyal to her chief," Pike said, "as you are yourself."

"She will go to He-cox whenever he wants her," Strong Bear said.

"Well," Pike said, "that might work in our favor."

"How could that be?" Strong Bear looked at Pike doubtfully.

Pike began talking, and Strong Bear was soon nodding his head in agreement . . .

CHAPTER EIGHT

"There is another white man in camp," Little Doe said to Hecox.

"Another white man?" he asked. He looked up from between her legs, where he had been kissing her belly. He'd been pleasantly surprised tonight; she had participated a lot more in their lovemaking. Instead of him making love to her, they had made love to each other. Only now did he suspect something was wrong.

"Who is this white man?"

"There are two," she said. "One is named Mack-onnel and the other one is Pike."

"Pike?"

"Do you know him?"

He looked up at her, resting his chin on her black pubic hair.

"I know of him," Hecox said, "but I don't know him."

"He says he knows you."

"Does he?"

"Well," she said, "he knows of you."

"Does he?" Hecox didn't know why Pike would have heard his name, but he was impressed by the fact that he had. "I wonder how he knows me?"

"He says you killed his squaw," Little Doe said, reaching down to tangle her fingers in Hecox's hair, "and burned down his house."

"What?" Hecox's head jerked up, and she accidentally pulled his hair. "Ow!"

He sat up quickly, slapping her hand away.

"What the hell are you talking about?"

"He says you and four other men killed his wife, and raped her, and burned down his house," she said. "He says he is going to kill you."

"Where'd you hear this from?"

"I told you," she said, "I heard it in camp."

Hecox stood up and began to pull on his pants, his face a mask of puzzlement. Little Doe watched him with pleasure, enjoying his confusion. She was lying there, her lovely body naked, and he wasn't paying her the least bit of attention.

"How would he know where to find me?" Hecox said, talking to himself.

"I heard," Little Doe said, "that he has already killed one of your friends."

"Who?" Hecox demanded.

"A man name . . . Hay-wood?"

"He got Haywood?"

"And Hay-wood told him that you would be here."

"That sonofabitch!"

Hecox pulled on his shirt and started pacing

the inside of the tent.

"Sonofabitch," he muttered again.

"Do you not want to make love anymore?" she asked.

"No!" he snapped. "Get up and get out, bitch."

Little Doe stood up, got dressed, and started to leave.

"Will you want me again later?"

"I won't be here later," he said. "Get out."

After Little Doe left, Hecox continued to pace the tent. If he stayed in camp, would Black Cherry Joe let Pike kill him? Sure he would. He'd take advantage of the opportunity to get rid of him, no matter what Walking Fawn said.

He had to get out of camp, and he had to do it without anyone seeing him.

Shit, he never should have let that little bitch leave. He should have broken her neck and left her here. She might tell somebody he was leaving.

He put on his moccasins and collected his gear. He stuck his head out of the teepee and saw that the camp was quiet. It was still dark and the sun wouldn't be coming up for a couple of hours. He could sneak to the horses in the dark and get out before anyone knew he was gone. He had to find Raitt and the others — only thing was he didn't know where Raitt was. But he knew where Murphy was hiding out. He'd find Murphy, and see if the big man knew where to locate Raitt.

He left the tent and hurried as quietly as he could to the horses. He left behind his own horse and took the best one he could find. He always rode without a saddle, anyway, so he simply threw a blanket up on the horse's back, climbed on, and walked the horse slowly out.

Fuck Pike, he thought, if he thought I was going to be an easy target.

Pike and Strong Bear both watched Hecox sneak through camp, mount up and ride out.

"It worked," Strong Bear said.

"Yes, it did."

"He is gone," the brave said.

"And he won't be coming back," Pike said, "I can guarantee that."

Strong Bear looked at Pike and said, "Kill him slowly."

"I will."

"Do you want help?"

Pike shook his head.

"We can handle it, Strong Bear," he said. He put his hand out and the other man took it. "Thank you for the help you have given me."

"And for your help in ridding us of him," Strong Bear said. "Walking Fawn will never know that he is dead, only that he never returns."

"And he won't," Pike said. "I promise."

McConnell and Buck were waiting in the teepee for Pike.

"Did it work?" McConnell asked.

"He just rode out," Pike said, collecting his gear. "Let's go."

"Pike," McConnell said, "why don't we leave the boy here?"

"No!" Buck said. "I want to come with you!"

"Buck—" McConnell said, but Pike cut him off.

"Skins," he said, "they won't want him. They won't accept him anymore than they accepted Hecox, and Buck won't have the protection of Black Cherry Joe. Right now he's better off with us."

McConnell looked down at the boy, who was still staring up at him, "Ah, I guess you're right. All right, boy, make yourself useful and carry something."

Happily, Buck grabbed an armful of McConnell's gear and the three of them left the teepee.

It was light by the time they stopped riding.

"He's in a hurry," McConnell said, studying the signs left by Hecox. "He's not bothering to try and hide his trail."

"He probably thinks he's got hours on us," Pike said.

"He's a half hour ahead of us, at most."

"We'll catch him before that," Pike said, touching his knife.

"Are you just gonna kill him?" McConnell asked.

Pike turned and looked at his friend, who was chilled by the coldness in the big man's eyes.

"What should I do, Skins?" he asked. "Give him a chance to explain? Maybe they had a reason for doing what they did?"

"There couldn't be a reason," McConnell said.

"Well then there couldn't be a reason for me not to kill him," Pike said, "could there?"

CHAPTER NINE

Allan Hecox was not in a very good frame of mind.

How were they to know that the Crow squaw was Jack Pike's woman? And even if they had known, would that have made a difference to Raitt? Bert Raitt was close to the craziest man he'd ever met.

Hecox knew where Mitch Murphy was, and that was where he was headed. Maybe between them they could figure out where he was Raitt was, if Murphy didn't know already. It was a pretty sure bet, though, that Pike was already tracking him. Maybe he and Murphy could lay a trap for Pike and kill him. If not, they could let Raitt figure out what to do about Pike.

If Allan Hecox were a braver man, he would never have thought about exposing his partners to Jack Pike. But the thought never entered his mind that he might handle Jack Pike alone. All he knew was that he needed help, and right at that moment, the only person he could think to help him was big Mitch Murphy.

Maybe Murphy could even take care of Pike himself?

Hecox could lead Pike to Murphy, and in the meantime get far enough away so that even if Pike killed Murphy, he'd lose Hecox?

After all, his own life was a hell of a lot more important that Mitch Murphy's, Dan Tilson's, or anyone else's.

Wasn't it?

Mitch Murphy was a big man. There wasn't a man Murphy knew—or had ever known—that he couldn't beat fair and square in a fist fight—and if fair and square didn't do it, down and dirty did.

Murphy picked up pocket change fighting; his face attested to that. It was marked with scars and swellings that had left it permanently deformed. In his late thirties, Murphy wasn't the smartest man in the world, which was why he needed people like Bert Raitt. Before Raitt came along, all of Murphy's money had been made with his fists. He'd take on all comers in a camp, a settlement, or at a rendezvous, and bet on himself every time.

Murphy didn't have to do that now. Not after Raitt had set up that sweet score over by Ham's Fork on the Bear River. Sure, they'd had to kill a bunch of people, but they walked away with nearly two hundred dollars each. To Mitch Murphy, two hundred dollars was a lot of money.

On Raitt's orders to hide out, Mitch Murphy had headed for a small encampment he knew of in the northern part of the Yellowstone, near the

72

Big Horn River, not far from Lisa's Fort. The people who lived there were off the beaten path, and way behind when it came to receiving news. They'd know nothing of what Raitt and Murphy and the others had done, not unless he told them, and not even Murphy was dumb enough to do that.

He'd been in camp for a number of weeks already and had only had three or four fights, and those had only been for fun. Now that the others had seen what he could do, they pretty much left him alone, and that was just fine with him. All he needed was two or three poker players, and a woman, and he was happy. He had all of that right where he was.

He was content to spend the month in the small encampment just as Raitt had instructed. Nothing could budge him.

Or so he thought.

"He figures he's being trailed," McConnell said. He had dismounted and was studying the ground.

"I know," Pike said. "He ain't moving in such a straight line, anymore. That ain't gonna buy him much time, though. We'll catch him."

"There's another way to do this, you know," McConnell said, mounting up again.

"Keep talking!"

"Well, we could just trail him and see who he leads us to."

"Can't do that," Pike said, shaking his head.

"Why not?"

"Couple of reasons."

"Name 'em."

"Well, for one he might lead us to all of them, and then we'd be outnumbered."

"And?"

"We don't know how far he's got to go," Pike said, "and we might lose him along the way."

"You and me lose a trail?"

"There's a first time for everything, Skins."

"You just want to kill him."

"I want to kill him so bad," Pike said, hiding nothing from his friend, "I can taste it."

"Pike—"

"You ain't never had this kind of bloodlust, Skins," Pike said, cutting his friend off. "You don't know what it's like."

"You're right about that," McConnell said. "I ain't never had it, and I hope I never do." He looked at his friend quickly and turned away. "I ain't criticizin', mind you—"

"I know it," Pike said quietly.

"So we're just gonna take him?"

"As soon as we can," Pike said.

McConnell shrugged. "You're callin' it, but what if he don't know where any of the others are?"

"A pack like he runs with," Pike said, "he's bound to know where one of them is, at least, just like Haywood did. They got to be able to get back together if something happens."

"Like somebody chasin' 'em down to kill them all?"

"Yeah," Pike said, "like that."

Hecox was tired, but he dared not stop. He didn't know for sure how many hours he had on his pursuers, but he knew it was safest to assume

74

that he didn't have more than two or three at the most.

Well, maybe with a two or three hour lead he could at least stop for some water.

He dismounted near a stream and let his horse drink. Then he got down on his belly to take a drink himself. When he laid himself flat on the ground he realized just how tired he really was. His bones ached and his eyes wanted nothing more than to close.

He took a drink and then rolled over onto his back. Just for a minute, he told himself, just for a minute . . .

"There he is," McConnell said.

"I see him."

They were on a rise above Hecox, who was still lying on his back next to the stream.

"He looks like he's dead," McConnell said.

"He ain't," Pike said, with certainty. "His chest's moving up and down."

"Let's go down and get him, then."

"No," Pike said. "You and the boy go on ahead, just in case he gets by me."

McConnell studied Pike for a moment. He realized that his friend didn't want the boy to see what he was going to do to the man, and probably didn't want Skins to see it, either. Maybe, McConnell thought, if he stayed, Pike wouldn't be able to do it — but he dismissed that thought. Pike might find it harder to do with McConnell watching, but he'd do it anyway. Nothing would stop him.

"All right," he finally said. "Buck and I will

75

ride ahead and make camp. We'll have something cooked up for you when . . . when you're done."

Pike nodded, and turned his horse.

"Be careful," McConnell said.

Pike nodded again and rode off. That cold look had come into the big man's eyes again, and he was beyond speaking.

He was concentrating on the grim work ahead.

Allan Hecox didn't fall asleep, but he might as well have. In fact, he might as well have died, for all the good his little rest did him.

Hecox opened his eyes when Pike's right foot thudded into his right side.

"Owww!" he yelled and rolled over, covering his side with both hands. He stayed that way a few seconds, and then looked around wildly to see who had kicked him.

"Who—who are you?" he asked, haltingly. He was still wincing from the pain in his side.

"You know who I am, Hecox."

Hecox looked up at the big man towering over him. He was well over six feet, wide shouldered and narrow-hipped, with a full beard and mustache.

"Are you . . . Pike?"

"See?" Pike said. "You do know who I am."

Pike kicked Hecox in the small of the back before the man could say another word and Hecox howled again, rolling over on the ground. When he had rolled onto his back, Pike drove his knee into the man's chest, pinning him to the ground. He put his left hand on the man's throat, and used his right hand to show Hecox his knife.

"Now, before I skin you alive, you're going to give me some names."

"I — I can't breathe . . ."

"You aren't going to have to worry about breathing much longer, Hecox so don't sweat it."

"You . . . you ain't gonna . . . just kill me . . . are you?"

"I am," Pike said, "but how long it takes, and how painful it is depends on you."

"Let's . . . let's make a deal," Hecox said. "I can give you one man, but you gotta let me go."

"I'll make a deal with you, but it's not that one," Pike said. "See, the question of you livin' ain't up for discussion. You're a dead man, but you can die easy, or you can die hard. You give me the man's name, and where to find him, and I'll kill you fast."

"Jesus . . . that's no deal!"

To illustrate that it was a deal, and the best one Hecox was going to get, Pike stretched out the man's right arm and drove the point of his knife right through Hecox's hand, staking it to the ground.

The scream that followed was like that of a wild animal . . .

McConnell and Buck both heard the scream as they started the campfire. McConnell looked off in the direction of the scream and then turned back to Buck.

"Pike is part Indian?" Buck asked.

"No," McConnell asked, "he's not. Why?"

"It is the Indian way to torture."

"Well, it's not the white man's," McConnell

said, and then looked off in the distance again and said, "not usually."

"Oh Christ, that hurts . . ." Hecox cried.

Pike pulled the knife free, but he would not let Hecox cradle his injured hand.

"If you move," Pike said, "I'll do the same thing to your left hand."

Hecox closed his eyes, squeezing out the tears, but he did not move.

"Now," Pike said, putting all of his weight to the man's chest again, "I'm going to make this very easy for you. The other three are Murphy, Tilson and Raitt. Which of them are you going to give me?"

"Jesus—" Hecox said, biting his bottom lip. "My hand—"

"I'll cut it clean off, next," Pike said, and the man's eyes went wide.

"Y-you won't," Hecox said. "W-without me you won't find any of the—the others. You can't kill me."

"I'm going to kill you, all right," Pike said, "but it's going to take a very long time, and in the end you'll give me what I want and *beg* me to kill you."

Hecox's face turned purple with rage and fear and he shouted, "You can't do this! You got no right!"

"Did you have a right to rape my woman? To kill her, and burn down our home?"

"She was a Crow squaw! That's all she was!"

"That's not all she was to me," Pike said.

His left hand moved toward Hecox's face and

the man jerked his head away. Pike wasn't reaching for his head, however, but for the man's left ear, and in turning his head Hecox had exposed it nicely.

Pike took hold of the ear and cut it cleanly off.

For a moment Hecox couldn't even scream, but then Pike held the ear for him to see letting the blood drip down onto the man's face and when Hecox opened his mouth to scream, Pike pushed the severed flesh into his mouth.

Hecox retched and Pike pushed the man's face aside, both to keep from getting puked on and to keep the man from drowning in his own vomit.

He wasn't ready to kill him.

Not just yet.

McConnell and Buck heard another blood-curdling scream and then they heard no more. McConnell put coffee on, and bacon, and Buck simply sat on a rock and watched for Pike.

Suddenly, the boy stood up, but didn't speak, and McConnell knew that Pike was coming.

Pike dismounted and Buck took his horse from him. As McConnell handed his friend a cup of coffee he could see the blood on Pike's shirt as well as on his face, and hands.

Pike set the coffee aside "I've got to wash up."

Pike spilled some water from a canteen onto his hands, rubbed the blood off, and then washed his face.

"Is it all off?" he asked.

"Yes," McConnell said, disapproval evident in the one word.

"We'll have Buck refill the canteen before we

leave," Pike said, setting it aside and picking up his coffee.

"And when will that be?" McConnell asked.

"In the morning."

"Where are we headed?"

"To an encampment on the Big Horn River, not far from Lisa's Fort."

"And who will we find there?"

"A man named Mitch Murphy," Pike said. "He's going to be number three."

PART TWO

AND THEN
THERE WERE THREE

CHAPTER TEN

Ten Days Later . . .

Mitch Murphy tossed his money into the pot and said, "Call." He would have raised again, but he remembered Raitt telling him not to throw too much money around.

The man seated across from him spread his cards on the table face-up and said, "Three threes."

Murphy whooped and set down his three Jacks.

"I ain't never seen a man so lucky," the other man said as Murphy raked in his winnings. It was the biggest pot of the night, twenty dollars.

"Just remember one thing, Murphy," the third player said.

"What's that, Grissom?"

"Your luck's gotta change."

"Maybe so," Murphy said, gathering up the cards for his deal, "but not tonight."

The big man was right. His luck wouldn't change until the next day . . . when Jack Pike rode in.

* * *

"You want breakfast?" McConnell asked Pike.

"No," Pike said, "just coffee. I want to get an early start and get there by noon."

"And have him dead by one?"

Pike frowned across the fire at McConnell.

"Why are you digging at me about this, Skins?"

"Because I don't approve."

"Then why are you here?"

"Because you're my friend."

"Well, if I'm your friend, do me a favor and stop digging at me. Maybe in a few months I'll figure I didn't do the right thing, but right now it feels as right as can be. Can't you accept that?"

"I guess I'll have to."

Pike drank half the coffee, then dumped the other half onto the fire.

"Let's get going. Where's the kid?"

"Loadin' up the mule."

"What are you going to do with him when we're done?" Pike asked.

"What do you mean?"

"Well, it's obvious he's taken a shine to you," Pike said. "Are you going to play daddy to him when this is all over?"

"Me? Daddy?"

"Well, what would you call the way you been acting of late?" Pike asked. "Not only have you been daddying him, but me, too."

"I ain't nobody's daddy," McConnell said, grumpily. "When this is all over we'll find him a home someplace."

"You'd be better off bringing him back to his own people."

"What if he don't want to go?"

Pike shrugged.

"Do you think you're going to find some white folks somewhere who will want him?"

McConnell hesitated a moment. "I don't rightly know, Pike. Look, I don't know now what I'm gonna do, but I don't think I got to think about that right now. Let's wait until this thing *is* all over, and then I'll figure it out."

"Well," Pike said, "that's up to you." He stood up and stamped out the rest of the fire, then spread the ashes around.

The sky was a crystal clear blue when they set out and there was nothing to stop them from making the settlement before noon.

This time Pike figured to size up the man and the situation some before he did anything. He'd been pretty lucky with the first two. But he wasn't as sure what kind of situation he was going to have to deal with this time, and he intended to take the time to find out.

Murphy woke up that morning and reached for the woman next to him.

He'd found Flora the second day he was in camp. Mitch Murphy was no raving beauty, that was damned sure, and by the same token, neither was Flora Griffin.

Most of the men at the encampment either had wives or squaws. When Murphy arrived he'd found very few unattached women, and the ones that were available were older than he was by a good number of years.

And then there was Flora.

He noticed her right away because she had the kind of body he preferred. Being a big man, he liked big women, and she sure fit that bill. From behind, he saw that she was tall, damn near six feet, wide-hipped and thick-waisted. She was more woman than most men could handle.

But not for Murphy.

He stared over at her snoring bulk sleeping naked in the bed beside him and once again felt the stirring of his penis. Their loving last night had been hot and sweaty, just the way he liked it, and she had taken her pleasure with almost as much physical ardor as he did. The memory of their rutting had him fully erect in no time.

Reaching over, he slapped at her huge haunch and she stirred sleepily.

Murphy grinned and grabbed one of her pendulous breasts, giving it a hard squeeze. "How about it Flora," the big man said, rubbing his hardened penis against her pillowy thigh.

"Mmmm," she murmured, lazily lifting one big leg over him, "but I could be more awake."

She sat up and he slid into her as easy as if she were butter. She leaned over so that her huge breasts were hanging right in front of his face and he sucked on them while she rode him.

She had smiled down at him. "I ain't had me a man in a month of Sundays who didn't complain that I was crushing the life out of him when I ride him like this."

"Honey," he said, with great satisfaction, "you can ride me like this anytime."

She rode him now, hard, so hard that she had to sit up and brace her hands on his hard belly while she bounced up and down. He watched the way

86

her breasts flopped and her hair swirled, and the way she bit her lip when her time came. The inside of her felt like a wet, warm glove and he let out a huge groan as she yanked the seed from him.

Seconds later she lay down on his chest, spent and said, "I never thought I'd find a man big enough to take me."

"You ain't so hard to take."

"Ha!" she said, sliding off him. "Ain't another man in camp who would even try me, because of the way I look. They all want them skinny, dark-skinned, pretty-faced squaws, not some oversized, ugly white woman."

"You know what I think?"

"What?"

"I think they was all scared of you."

She looked up at him and, smiling, said, "Yeah? You really think so?"

"I do. I think they was all scared that you'd break them, or something. There ain't a man in camp who could handle a real woman like you, Flora."

"Until now," she said, rubbing up against him.

"Damned right, until now," he said, reaching for her.

When Pike, McConnell and Buck rode into the camp they found just about what they had expected. Ramshackle tents scattered about in no particular order. There wasn't a more permanent structure to be seen, and the only thing in the camp even made of wood was an old lean-to used to shelter powder from the weather.

Off to one side, the horses were picketed, and they rode over to picket their own animals.

From the number of animals they saw, there were apparently twenty or twenty-five people in the camp, and most of these were men. What women they did see were busy cooking, or doing laundry, or mending clothes.

In general the three of them attracted little attention, except for Pike. As big as he was, he drew appraising looks from men and women alike. Pike was a man who demanded a proper amount of attention — and respect. More than one woman licked her lips as he walked by, then glanced around guiltily to see if her man had seen.

"What do we do now?" McConnell asked.

"Even a camp this size has to have a booshway," Pike said. "Let's find him and see if we can get something to eat. If not, we'll just have to stake out a spot and make a meal for ourselves."

That turned out to be unnecessary, though, because a moment later Pike saw someone he recognized.

"Is that Pete Davis?"

"Where?" McConnell asked, looking around.

Pike pointed. "Right there."

McConnell looked where his friend was pointing. "Damned if it ain't Cockeyed Davis."

"Don't let him hear you say that," Pike said.

Pete "Cockeyed" Davis was an acquaintance of theirs who was a little bit sensitive about the fact that he had no control over his left eye. It seemed to wander around in its socket of its own accord, and more than one person had found it worthy of comment while they were talking to Pete. Pete, however did not take well to jokes — or even questions—about his eye, and more than once a tactless comment had led to trouble.

Someone once had the nerve to ask Pete why he always tried to bite his opponent's ear off in a fight.

"Let them walk around with one ear and have people staring at them, or commenting about it all the time, and see how it feels," was his reply.

"Pete!" Pike called out. "Peter Davis?"

Davis, who had been cleaning his rifle, looked up and squinted against the sunlight to see who was calling his name.

"Who's that?"

"It's Jack Pike, Pete."

"Pike?"

"And Skins McConnell."

Pike allowed McConnell and Buck to go ahead of him, and stood farther back, so that Davis wouldn't have to look up quite so high to talk to him. Pike had found that short men were always resentful of men of Pike's height.

"What the hell are you two doin' up this way?" Davis asked, standing up.

"Well, right now we're looking to see if we can't get a meal," McConnell said. "Who's the booshway of this camp?"

"Napoleon Bonet," Davis said, "but don't bother looking for him, he went out this morning hunting. You don't need him, though. I'll have my woman cook up something extra. Set and take a load off."

"Thanks, Pete."

Pike sat, which put him on more equal terms with Pete Davis.

Pete Davis' woman turned out to be a Nez Perce

squaw somewhat older than him, but not unattractive. She also turned out to be a decent cook, and even made a decent pot of coffee. Of course, she was also a few inches taller than Davis, but the man didn't seem to mind it so much in women, only men. After all, a woman was a woman. No matter how tall she was, she was still going to serve her man.

At one point, when Davis went off to talk to his squaw, Pike and McConnell had discussed quickly whether or not to tell Davis about Mitch Murphy. They decided that since they had Buck along, they'd just wait for the boy to point the man out. To that end McConnell warned Buck that when he did see the man he was to let them know, but not to make it obvious.

"How long have you been out this way?" McConnell asked.

"Oh, a number of months now," Davis said. "When I got here there were only three or four others and I decided to stay a spell. People keep comin' in the way they been, though, and we'll have to put up a trading post, or something."

"Been gettin' a lot of people lately?"

"Well," Davis said, "one fella came in last month, and now you fellas."

"The fella who came in last month," McConnell asked. "Did he stay?" It was the same question that had come to Pike's mind, and he was pleased that McConnell had asked it.

"Yeah, he stayed. Took up with a woman, too. Still don't know if he's stayin' for good, though." Davis looked at McConnell and asked, "Why you so interested?"

McConnell shrugged. "Just makin' conversation

90

until the food is ready."

"Speakin' of conversation," Davis said, "why you draggin' the Indian boy around with you?"

McConnell shrugged.

"Don't rightly know. We came across him last month and he just sort of stayed with us. I guess we're looking for someplace to leave him."

"You could leave him here," Davis said. "Between me and the missus we got plenty of work for him."

McConnell looked at Buck, who was staring at him with big, brown eyes. "I guess we'll have to think on that a spell."

"Think away," Davis said. "Here comes the food, and the way this gal of mine cooks we ain't gonna be talkin' for a spell."

Davis was right. The food was so good that none of them spoke another word until they were through.

CHAPTER ELEVEN

After they finished eating they thanked Pete Davis and his wife for their hospitality and went in search of Mitch Murphy.

"You played that perfectly," Pike told McConnell. "This fella Murphy hasn't been here long enough to make close friends. All we have to do is have Buck point him out, and he'll be mine."

"I don't know about that," McConnell said, "a small camp like this, the people can be pretty close. I think we ought to move cautiously, Pike."

Pike considered his friend's word for a few moments and then nodded.

"I hate to admit it, but you're probably right."

Pike put his hand on McConnell's arm to stop him.

"Look, now that you've got me thinking straight, there's no point in all three of us traipsing through camp. Since we're going to have to spend at least one night here, one of us might as well set up camp."

"I suggest that you do it."

"Why me?"

"Two reasons," McConnell said. "One, you attract more attention than I do, just because of your size."

"Yeah?"

"And second, when you find Murphy, you may not be able to control yourself."

"Skins—"

"Besides," McConnell said, cutting Pike off, "Buck will feel more comfortable with me."

Pike opened his mouth to argue, then abruptly shut it.

"All right," he said, "I'll pitch camp—but you come and let me know the minute you find him."

"I will," McConnell said, and he watched as Pike walked away toward their horses.

Buck and McConnell strolled from one end of the camp to the other but they saw no sign of Murphy. McConnell figured that the man was either off hunting, or inside his tent with the woman Pete Davis had spoken about.

Of course, there was another possibility, but McConnell preferred not to think about that. He didn't know how Pike would react if it turned out that Mitch Murphy *wasn't* in camp. The big man was right on the edge now; that kind of disappointment just might push him over it.

McConnell was still walking and thinking this when Buck suddenly grabbed his wrist, stopping him. He looked down at the Crow boy, and then followed his gaze.

There was a man coming out of a tent, followed by a woman. McConnell noticed that the woman was big, full-bodied and darkhaired. She reminded him that he'd been without a woman far too long, traveling with Pike on this ride for vengeance. The woman did not have an attractive face, but it was flushed and it was obvious to anyone with eyes what she and the man had been up to in the tent. Reluctantly McConnell dragged his eyes from the full-sized woman to look at her man.

Mitch Murphy was a hulking brute. His size made him an obvious match for the woman, and his face was even uglier. It had been pounded by too many fists over the years and was a mass of lumps and scars.

If it were possible, Murphy was even larger than Pike. Although Pike might have matched the man in the width of his shoulders and the breadth of his chest, this man was thicker through the waist and hips, and had legs like tree trunks. Just looking at the man, McConnell would have to give Murphy the edge in raw power.

He doubted that Mitch Murphy would fall as easily as Haywood and Hecox had.

McConnell moved Buck away from the tent, so the man would not see them staring at him.

"Is that him, Buck?"

The Crow boy nodded, his brown eyes wide and sincere.

"He is one of them," Buck said. "I am sure."

"All right," McConnell said. "Let's get back to Pike and let him know that we've found him."

They started off in search of the camp Pike would have pitched by now.

"Pike will kill him?"

"Yes, I'm sorry to say, Pike will kill him."

"Why are you sorry?" Buck asked. "For what

94

they did, the men deserve to die. Do you not believe that?"

"Of course I believe it, Buck."

"Then why are you sorry?"

"Because Pike is my friend, and I don't like to see my friend in a killing frenzy."

"What is . . . frenzy?"

McConnell sought a word or phrase that the boy would understand.

"It is a bloodlust, Buck, a blood lust that consumes a man, turns him into something and someone he usually is not."

"Pike will not be the same man when he is finished?"

"No, he will not."

Buck thought a moment, his brow furrowed, and then said, "Then I am sad, too."

McConnell put his hand on the boy's shoulder as they headed back to find Pike.

"Did you see that?" Mitch Murphy asked.

"See what?" Flora asked.

"A white man and an Indian boy," Murphy said. "They was looking at us."

He was about to wash up in a basin of water when he spotted the two looking their way. But they had disappeared.

"Do you think it's that obvious?" Flora asked.

"Is what that obvious?"

"What we've been doing in the tent."

Murphy looked at Flora and saw that she was glowing.

"They can't tell nothin' from lookin' at me, girl,

but your face . . ."

She touched her cheek, and her chin, and asked, "What's wrong with my face?"

"It's beautiful, Flora," Murphy said, "it's damn beautiful," and he forgot all about the man and the boy.

Pike reacted as McConnell knew he would.

"Show me," he said.

"Not yet."

"Why not?"

"Not until you get that look out of your eyes."

"What look?"

"Bloodlust."

They both looked down at Buck, who had spoken the word.

"Keep quiet, boy," Pike said, and Buck looked hurt.

"Pike, this one is different from the other two."

"How?"

"Well, for one thing he's as big as you are, and heavier."

"So you think I should back off because I'm going up against a bigger man?"

"No, I'm not saying that. What I am saying is that you should be more careful with this one."

Pike stared at his friend a moment, and then shrugged.

"All right, I understand what you're saying. And you," Pike added, looking at Buck, "I'm sorry for the way I spoke to you."

"Do not worry," Buck said. "We are your friends. We will help you."

Pike rumpled the boy's hair and said, "I know you are, Buck." He looked at McConnell and said, "I'll take a look at Murphy a little later on."

"How?"

"Well, you'll describe him to me and I'll go for a little walk."

"We'll go with you," McConnell said.

"We tried that already and we attracted too much attention. No, I'll go alone. You don't have to worry about me. I'll keep a cool head."

McConnell studied his friend's face, wanting nothing more than to believe him.

"Don't worry, Skins," Pike said again, "I can control myself."

Later on, Pike went for his walk. McConnell was still nervous about letting Pike go out on his own, but he knew there was no use trying to talk his friend out of it.

What McConnell did not know was that Pike was as nervous—even *more* nervous—than he was. Pike was not at all sure that he would be able to keep his word about controlling himself. Oh, he had every intention of *trying* to keep his word, but when he thought about what Murphy and his friends had done to Sun Rising . . . when he thought about the way Sun Rising looked lying on the ground, battered and burned, he felt that he owed it to her to kill these men on sight, the way you would kill a mad dog, or a crazed wolf, or any other sick animal.

And then there was the guilt . . .

He had been trying to deal with the guilt ever

since her death. He knew that she had loved him, but he didn't think that he had ever really loved her, and she had deserved better. She had deserved to be loved in a way he could never have loved her . . . and he didn't know why he hadn't loved her. He couldn't figure it out. She was everything any man could ever have wanted. She was loving, in bed and out, she was kind, gentle, a wonderful cook . . .

He convinced himself that there was something wrong with him for not being able to love her. Maybe, in his own way, he too was sick, and Sun Rising had paid the price for crossing the path of not five sick men, but six.

Maybe he was as much to blame for her death as they were.

And maybe by killing them, he was also punishing himself.

The old Jack Pike would never have considered taking of five human lives to be a small thing, but he was no longer the same man. He was now a new Jack Pike, a man single-minded in his quest for revenge and, perhaps most importantly his quest for forgiveness.

So he took his walk, following the directions McConnell had given him. The men and women of the camp watched him, but none dared to approach. Pike didn't know it, but his appearance during this blood hunt of his was at once foreboding and frightening. He looked for all the world like a man who would kick a dog, or a small child, if either of them dared to cross his path.

98

He spotted the tent, recognizing it by McConnell's description, but he suddenly found himself at a loss for what to do. He couldn't simply stand outside the tent, waiting for the man to come out. He decided to walk close by the tent and see if he could learn anything.

As he passed by, he noticed several things. The flap of the tent was closed, apparently tied shut but there were wet clothes hanging outside. The size of the shirt and pants were in keeping with McConnell's description of the man who had worn them; a small table was sitting under a makeshift canopy of blankets that had been rigged in front of the tent, and on the table were a couple of decks of cards. They were stacked, but the stacks had fallen over, and both decks were mixed. The cards appeared to be well worn; lastly, there was a murmur of voices from inside the tent, the voices of a man and a woman.

Pike's sharp eye took all of this in as he walked past. He wondered how he was going to make another pass by the tent without attracting attention when the flap was suddenly thrown back.

A man and a woman appeared in the entrance, embraced briefly, and then the woman left. The man watched her walk away, and Pike noticed that she had a body that would bear watching, but he had no eyes for the woman now, he only had eyes for the man.

This was his first look at Mitch Murphy, the third of the five men who had raped and killed Sun Rising, and burned down his home. He felt a lump rise in his throat, and heat formed behind his eyes. The man was barechested, and massive, as McConnell had said, but Pike was tempted to walk up to him and kill him where he stood.

He couldn't do that, however; it had nothing to do with his promise to Skins.

Before Mitch Murphy could die — before Pike would allow him to die — he had to tell Pike where he could find one or both of the other men.

Pike would know no peace unless he succeeded in killing all five.

When Pike returned to camp McConnell noticed that his friend's face had a new and terrible look to it. The eyes were hard and cold, his jaw set so firmly that the muscles in his cheeks were quivering. His shoulders were hunched, his arms held stiffly at his sides, both hands balled into fists.

"You saw him," McConnell said.

"Yes."

"Did you — "

"I didn't do anything," Pike said, sitting opposite McConnell. "I just looked at him."

"Pike — "

"I wanted to kill him," Pike went on, "but he has to talk to me first."

McConnell didn't say anything.

"Then he dies."

McConnell watched his friend closely, waiting for him to speak again. When he didn't, he assumed that Pike had said all he had to say.

"I suppose we'll have to figure out a way to approach him."

After a moment's hesitation, Pike said, "I think I've thought of a way."

"How?"

Pike looked at McConnell and asked, "Who's a better poker player, me or you?"

CHAPTER TWELVE

Later that night, Pike and McConnell left Buck asleep and walked back into camp. Pike had pitched their tent well away from any of the others, so that they were really too far away to be considered part of the main camp at all. Pike preferred it that way, and felt that the members of the camp would too, at least until the newcomers had made their intentions known.

And, once their intentions *were* known, it was doubtful that anyone would even want them as part of the camp.

Pike had explained to McConnell what he had seen outside of Mitch Murphy's tent.

"Damn," McConnell had said, "I didn't see half of that, and we were seeing the same things."

"Never mind," Pike said. "You did a fine enough job just describing the man."

McConnell frowned. "He's big, isn't he?"

"Like a grizzly, but remember how many grizzlies we've put down this year?"

"I'd rather not."

Pike explained that from the look of the well-worn playing cards he'd seen, Murphy was an avid poker player.

"Unless he likes solitaire," McConnell had suggested.

"Well," Pike said, "if he's a solitaire player, we'll just have to figure something else out."

The first thing they had to do was establish that there *was* a poker game going in camp. For that they decided to rely on Pete Davis.

They walked to Davis' tent, but found that he wasn't there. When they asked his wife where he was, she answered two questions at once.

"He is at the poker game."

Pike could barely contain himself.

"Ma'am, could you tell us where the game is at?"

"You want to play?"

"Yes."

The woman squinted at Pike, deepening the lines around her eyes, until they looked as if they had been etched there. "Good. Maybe you get some money back from the big man."

"Big man?" Pike said.

"Murphy," she said, her tone plainly showing her distaste. "Big white man, take money from everyone in poker. You beat him?"

"I can try."

"I tell you where game is."

She told them to go to the tent of a man called Lemuel Simmons, and gave them directions.

"Will they let us play?" McConnell asked.

"Probably not," she said, "but you tell big man you can beat him. Big winner control game, right?"

"That's the way it usually works," Pike said.

"Good," she said. "You go, you play, you beat big man and I cook you one hell of good meal."

In spite of the grimness he felt, Pike grinned at the woman and said, "You've got a deal."

They followed the woman's directions and found a well-lit tent with loud voices coming from inside, laughing, cajoling and cursing.

"I think this is the place," McConnell said.

Pike nodded, and they went to the tent flap and peered inside. A blanket had been spread out on the floor of the tent, and there were money and cards on it. Four men were seated around the blanket, playing poker, and there were several peering over their shoulders, watching them.

When Pike and McConnell entered, every eye in the tent turned to them.

The man who spoke, however, was Lem Simmons.

"Can we help ya?"

"Yeah," McConnell said, "we heard there was a poker game in progress."

"So?" Simmons was a ruddy-faced man in his fifties who looked as if he were always in bad humor — or maybe he just looked that way because he was losing.

"So . . . we'd like to play."

"Both of ya?"

"No," McConnell said, "just my friend."

"Your friend got a name?"

"Pike." Pike answered.

"I know Pike," Peter Davis said. He was one of

104

the men standing and not playing.

"I heard of him, too," Simmons said, "but that don't mean he can play. Besides, this ain't your tent and you ain't even in the game, Davis."

"What about him?" Pike asked.

"Who?" Simmons asked.

"Him," Pike said, indicating Mitch Murphy. "He looks like he's the big winner."

"So?" Simmons asked.

"Maybe he'd like a little more competition than he's getting."

"Whataya mean—" Simmons started to say, but Pike cut him off.

"Maybe he'd like to play someone who can beat him."

"Who do you think—" Simmons started, but this time it was Murphy who cut him off.

"Let him play, Lem."

"What?"

Murphy stared hard at Simmons.

"Why don't you get up and give him your place, Lem?" Murphy said. "You ain't doin' so hot tonight."

Simmons was about to protest but the other players took Murphy's side.

"Come on, Lem," one of them said, "I'd like to see somebody beat Murphy for once."

"Come on, Lem," another man echoed, "I want to play another hand tonight."

Simmons gave them all cold stares, and then abruptly stood up and left the tent, storming past Pike and McConnell.

"Ain't this his tent?" McConnell asked.

"It don't matter whose tent we play in," Murphy

said, "ol' Lem usually ends up walking out." He smiled at Pike and said, "Take a seat, Pike, and let's play some poker."

Pike wanted to smash Murphy's face in, but he took his place on the floor, placed his money on the blanket, and said, "Deal."

In the first hour of play, Pike noticed two things about Mitch Murphy.

One, the man was not very intelligent.

Second, he was a good poker player.

This confused Pike, who'd always thought that he was a good poker player *because* he was intelligent.

But after several hands Pike realized that Murphy was a good poker player because he *wasn't* intelligent. When the man played, he played with the singleminded concentration of a child, whose mind had not yet developed enough to be able to do two things at once. He did not play and hold a conversation with the other players, he simply concentrated on the game, while the other men played and talked.

It annoyed Pike to discover that Murphy was clearly a better poker player than he was.

If he was going to beat the man, he was going to have to break his concentration.

During the second hour Pike ignored the other players and talked constantly to Murphy. It didn't matter that Murphy rarely replied with more than a nod, or a shrug, or a grunt. What mattered was that the man was paying some attention to him, and that meant that he was paying that much less attention to his cards.

In the second hour, Murphy lost all that he had won the first hour—and more.

During the third hour, the other men were able to recoup some of their losses. For that reason they were all in good humor—even Simmons, who had returned to watch Murphy lose—everyone, that is, with the exception of Mitch Murphy.

He was in a decidedly foul mood.

Presently, Pike won a big hand of seven card stud after his incessant chatter had caused Murphy to incorrectly read the cards that Pike had on the table. Consequently, Pike was able to spring a winning hand on Murphy and take the largest pot of the night.

It was clear to Pike that Murphy hated to lose, which the man continued to do for most of the evening, until the game finally ended.

"You can't end the game," Murphy said. "I'm too far behind."

"Better luck next time," Lem Simmons said. Even the perpetually dour Simmons was smiling.

"No," Murphy said, refusing to move, "I want to win it back tonight."

McConnell immediately looked at Pike. Clearly, here was an ideal situation for a confrontation, and he could see that his friend was going to go right for it.

"Tonight's not your night, Murphy," Pike said. "Why don't you let it go at that?"

"It woulda been my night, if it hadn't been for you," Murphy groused.

"Remember," Lem Simmons said, "you're the one who wanted him to play."

"Shut up, Simmons!" Murphy said, harshly. "I coulda beat him if he'd've kept his mouth shut. I'm a better player than he is."

"I doubt," Pike said, very carefully, "that there's much of anything you are better at than I am, Murphy."

"Is that what you think, Pike?" Murphy demanded, standing up quickly.

Skins McConnell stepped in at that moment to help things along.

"Easy, Murphy," McConnell said, stepping between the two big men and laying a hand flat against Mitch Murphy's chest. "You don't want to get Pike mad. You wouldn't like him when he's mad."

Murphy's eyes burned into McConnell's.

"You think I'm afraid of him? Just because he's got a reputation?"

"I'm just sayin' you shouldn't start anything you can't finish."

Murphy became aware that everyone was watching him, and felt—as McConnell had intended him to feel—that he was being belittled.

With a roar he backhanded McConnell, brutally knocking him out of his way. He the charged mountain man and found himself looking down the barrel of Pike's Kentucky pistol.

It took all of Pike's will not to pull the trigger and blow the man's head off then and there.

Murphy, though in a rage, did not charge the drawn pistol.

"Sore loser?" Pike asked from behind the pistol.

"You're too much of a coward to face me man to man," Murphy said.

108

McConnell had regained his feet and was licking his bloody lip. Every man in the tent was studying Pike, to see what he would do next.

Pike glanced at McConnell, then lowered the pistol and stuck it in his belt.

"You name the where and when," he said.

"There's a clearing just north of the camp. Do you know it?"

Pike did. They were camped not far from it.

"I know it."

"Meet me there, at first light," Murphy said, "and we'll settle this."

"I'll be there."

Murphy looked around at the others, and then pushed past Pike and left.

"Can you beat him?" Pete Davis asked.

"We'll find out in the morning," Pike said.

"We hope you can," one of the other men said. "He's been using his size and strength to run roughshod over us since he arrived."

"Why didn't you put him out?" Pike asked.

"Ain't no one here been man enough to try," Lem Simmons said, "until you. I hope you break his neck."

Pike looked at McConnell, then back at Simmons and the others. "I'll see what I can do."

"You're beginning to surprise me," Pike said to McConnell as they walked back to their camp.

"How so?"

"You baited him perfectly. It was like you knew just what to say to him."

"He's a big man," McConnell said.

109

"And?"

"Big men have egos," McConnell said. "All you got to do is prod them a little."

Pike waited a moment, then said, "Present company excluded?"

Now it was McConnell's turn to hesitate. "I didn't say that," he grinned.

CHAPTER THIRTEEN

"You shouldn't do this," Flora said as Murphy prepared for his fight with Pike.

"Why not?" he demanded. "Don't you think I can beat Pike?"

"I don't know if you can or can't," she said. "I've heard of Pike. He has a reputation—"

He whirled on her angrily.

"I don't care about his reputation!" he shouted. "I can beat any man alive in a fight."

"Ohhh," she said, angrily, "you're so *dumb!*"

"Don't call me that."

She moved closer to him and shouted, "You let them bait you into this."

"What?" he said, staring at her blankly. "What are you talking about, bait?"

"They want to get rid of you," she said. "They think they've found someone who can beat you."

"Well, they haven't."

"Don't fight him, Mitch," she said. "If you're so sure you can beat him, then don't fight him."

He stared at her, frowning, and said, "I don't understand that."

111

"No," she said, sharply, "I know you don't. That's because you're so . . . damn . . . dumb."

"I told you not to call me that!" he shouted, and backhanded her across the mouth. The blow knocked her down, split her right cheek, and glazed her eyes.

By the time he was ready to leave the tent, she had regained her senses. She was still sitting on the floor, holding her hand to her bloody cheek, glaring at him.

"All right, go ahead, prove to yourself that you're a man, but whether you win or not, don't expect to find me here when you get back."

Murphy left without even looking at her again. She'd be there when he got back, all right. He gave her something nobody else could. She was a woman; she needed a man like him, and she knew it.

Why was she giving him such a hard time? Why didn't she understand that a man had to prove himself over and over again, or he wasn't a man? It was true that he wasn't a smart man, that all he could do was play cards and fight. Pike had beaten him at cards, so he had to fight him. It was as simple as that.

Even a woman should have been able to understand that.

Buck didn't ask any questions the next morning. He hadn't been as asleep as they had thought the night before and he'd heard them discussing what had happened.

"You're at a disadvantage," McConnell said.

"I know," Pike said, "but tell me, anyway."

112

"You don't want to kill him," McConnell said, "not until he tells you where to find the next man."

"Right."

Meantime he won't have any qualms about killing you."

"So?" Pike said.

"Pike, if he's gonna kill you, at some point you're going to have to make a decision. You might have to kill him to save your own life, whether or not he gives you the next man. Are you ready to do that?"

Pike looked at McConnell. "I won't be able to find the other two if I'm dead, now will I?"

"No," McConnell said, "you won't."

When Pike and McConnell reached the clearing, Murphy was already there along with a big crowd. Most of the camp had turned out to watch the giants collide.

Murphy was at the far end of the clearing, barechested. His torso was thick and covered with hair.

Pike removed his shirt, revealing a sculpted, hairless chest.

Both men had biceps like stone, but where Pike tapered to a slender waist, Murphy's body was thick all the way through.

The onlookers were sizing up the two men and busy making bets.

McConnell, never a man to miss an opportunity, went over to put some money down on Pike.

Buck, who had been told to stay back at camp, naturally did not. He appeared at Pike's side.

"Weren't you told to stay in camp?" Pike asked, noticing him.

"Did you expect me to?"

Pike grinned in spite of himself. "You're a pretty smart kid, aren't you?"

"If I had money, I would bet it on you."

"See?" Pike said. "You *are* a smart boy."

Buck suddenly looked worried. "Will you defeat him?"

Pike looked away from the Crow boy and stared across the clearing at Mitch Murphy.

"At least."

"What have you been doing?" Pike asked, when McConnell returned.

"Me? I've been betting some money on you."

"Some money?" Pike asked. "How much is some?"

"Oh, a lot."

"Do you think I need the added incentive?" Pike asked. "How much is a lot?"

"All of my money."

"I see."

"And yours."

"What?"

"Pay attention," McConnell said. "I think Murphy's about ready."

"Here," Pike said, handing McConnell his Kentucky pistol. "Anybody on that side of the clearing carrying a weapon?"

"I saw some knives, but no one has a gun."

"Has Murphy got any friends?"

"They're betting on him, but nobody claims to be his friend."

"Then why are they betting on him?"

"Well, they're betting on him because they *think* he's going to win, but they *hope* that you're going to win and that he'll leave."

"So they can't lose, huh?"

"No," McConnell said, "only you and Murphy can lose."

"Where's his woman?"

"I don't know," McConnell said, "but she's not here. All you have to worry about is him." McConnell pointed his finger at Murphy, across the clearing.

"Take Buck and move aside, Skins."

"It's cold," McConnell said, looking at the sky, "but at least you don't have to worry about snow. There'll be good footing beneath you."

"Move away, Skins."

"You're bound to be faster than he is," McConnell continued. "Use your speed—"

"Skins!"

"What?"

"Do you want to fight him?"

McConnell looked appalled.

"No!"

"Then move aside and let me get on with it."

"Come on, Buck," McConnell said. "Good luck, Pike."

As they were walking away, McConnell's hand on the boy's shoulders, Pike heard his friend say, "Hey, weren't you told to stay back in camp?"

The prelude to the fight was almost formal. The clearing itself formed a makeshift ring, and the spectators had moved around so that they

115

nearly ringed the entire clearing.

Murphy made the first move, striding toward Pike, and Pike advanced to meet him.

They faced each other almost dead center in the clearing, and McConnell could see that Pike was slightly taller, while Murphy was clearly heavier.

"Use your speed," McConnell said to himself, and suddenly Murphy swung . . .

It was a clumsy attempt to end the fight fast.

Murphy joined his hands and swung an axe-handle blow at Pike's head. Pike easily avoided the blow and struck Murphy in the mid-section. The blow was meant only to tell Pike what he wanted to know, just how hard Murphy's stomach was — and it was very hard. If he had the time Pike thought he could probably wear Murphy down with body blows, but he wanted to establish himself very quickly. He wanted to make an impression on Murphy.

Pike circled, causing his opponent to turn with him, and then waited for Murphy to strike.

Pete Davis had worked his way over to where McConnell was watching the action.

"Pike looks afraid."

"Don't bet on it."

"I already have," Davis said. "I think Murphy will take him apart."

"I don't have any more money or I'd make you put your money where your mouth is."

Davis looked past McConnell to where Buck was standing.

116

"You've got something even better than money," Davis said.

McConnell looked at Davis, and saw him looking at Buck. He looked down at the Crow boy, who smiled up at him with confidence and nodded.

"Maybe we can . . ." McConnell said.

Murphy ran out of patience and charged. Pike sidestepped, tripped the other man, and turned to watch him go down.

Murphy fooled him.

The thick man stumbled, but he did not fall. He regained his balance, turned, and swung. Pike moved his head to the side, but the blow struck him on the ear. Murphy's fist was so large and heavy that even the glancing blow made Pike's ear ring.

Pike backpedalled and tried to reassess the situation. Murphy was not fast, but he was not quite as clumsy as Pike had thought—and the time for him to take charge was rapidly passing.

This time, when Murphy charged him, he charged as well. When both men collided, more than a few of the onlookers—including Skins McConnell—winced at the impact.

CHAPTER FOURTEEN

Neither man budged.

The cords stood out on their necks, their arms swelled, their legs quivered, their feet dug for purchase. Their hands were locked, fingers laced, each straining against the strength and weight of the other.

Pike knew that Murphy's legs were thicker than his. The man had more weight in his middle. Pike could already feel his own leg muscles beginning to give. He had to do something before Murphy drove him back, or worse, drove him to his knees.

Abruptly, he stopped pushing. He stepped back and went down onto his back, pulling Murphy with him. Murphy, surprised, started to fall, but Pike brought his feet up, drove them into Murphy's midsection, and kicked out with all his strength.

Murphy was thrown clear over Pike's head and landed heavily on the ground behind him, raising a huge cloud of dust.

Moving with the speed of a cat, Pike was on him before Murphy could collect his wind, or regain his feet. He turned the man over, sliding his left arm beneath his chin, and pressing his left to the back of his head. Pike positioned his hands so that all he would have to do is twist, and even Murphy's thick neck would snap.

"All right, Murphy," Pike hissed into the other man's ear, "play time is over."

Murphy struggled, but Pike pressed his arm against the man's windpipe and held it there until he held still.

"Good, very good, Mitch," Pike said. "You learn fast. Now listen to me. You and four friends raped and killed my woman and burned my house. Do you remember that?"

"What are you—"

Pike cut off his air again and said, "We're not going to get anywhere if you keep interrupting me. Understand?"

Murphy nodded his head quickly.

"Good," Pike said, letting him breathe, "now let's start again . . ."

"What's going on?" Pete Davis asked. "What are they doing?"

"Can't you see?"

"I see two men on their knees," Davis said. He looked around, and the others also seemed puzzled by what was happening—or what *wasn't* happening. "What the hell are they doing?"

"Relax, Pete," McConnell said, "Pike is just wearing him down, is all . . ."

". . . answer my question. Do you remember?"

"Yes," Murphy said, "I remember. Shit, Pike, we didn't know she was yours. We thought she was just a—"

"Shut up!" Pike said. "Shut up and listen. Haywood is dead. I killed him at Clark's Fork. I blew his head off!"

"Wha—"

"He gave me Hecox. He's dead, too. I slit his throat, but not before he gave me you."

"You killed them both?"

"Both," Pike said, "and I'll kill you if you don't tell me where to find the other two."

"I can't—"

Pike turned Murphy's head so the man could feel the pressure on his neck.

"I can snap your neck with no problem, Murphy. You want that?"

"No, no," the man rasped. "Ease up!"

Pike eased the pressure.

"Give me a name."

"Pike, let's make a deal—"

"No deal, Murphy," Pike said. "Talk or die . . . now!"

He twisted Murphy's neck as far as he could without breaking it, and Murphy squealed, "All right, all right . . ."

"The name," Pike said.

"Tilson. Dan Tilson."

"Where?"

Murphy didn't answer, a last ditch effort at bravado. Pike twisted his neck again and Murphy cried out in pain.

"The Fort," Murphy said, "Lisa's Fort!"

"Good-bye, Murphy," Pike grated.

Murphy immediately knew what those words

meant.

"Pike, you said—"

"I lied, Mitch," Pike said, and twisted sharply.

McConnell saw Pike snap Murphy's head around, and saw the huge body go limp.

"What the hell—" Pete Davis said.

"You owe me money, Pete," McConnell said, "and so do a lot of other people."

They watched as Pike released Murphy and stood up. Murphy's body fell over, face down in the dirt.

"It's worth it," Davis said, "and I'm sure the others will agree."

"I'm sure they will," McConnell said, and he and Buck walked over to Pike.

Pike turned and looked at the stunned spectators. Then he put on the shirt Buck handed him.

"You could have made it look harder," McConnell said.

"I could have," Pike said, putting on his shirt.

"Where are we going from here?"

"To Lisa's Fort," Pike said. "The name is Tilson, Dan Tilson."

"I'll collect our money and we can break camp."

"Collect the money," Pike said, "but we can break camp in the morning. Lisa's Fort is not that far away."

"You're the boss," McConnell said.

While McConnell went to take care of business, Pike stood over the body of Mitch Murphy. He hadn't taken much pleasure in killing Murphy, and that bothered him. Not that he had taken pleasure in killing the other two, but with them he had not even been *aware* of the presence or lack of pleasure.

Perhaps his blood was not running as cold as it had three killings ago. Pike hoped that by the time he reached the fifth man he would still be able to do what had to be done.

Pike left the clearing and went straight to Murphy's tent. He didn't know if he'd find anything helpful there or not, but it seemed a pretty logical step to take.

He was going through Murphy's belongings when someone stepped into the tent behind him. He turned and saw the woman standing there — Murphy's woman. She was very tall, buxom and wide-hipped, with long dark hair. Her face was plain, but strong, not unappealing.

"Is it over?" she asked.

He wasn't quite sure what to say, and for a moment couldn't find his voice.

When he finally spoke he said, "Yes, it's over."

"He's dead?"

"I'm sorry."

"Don't be."

Pike frowned.

"I thought you were his woman?"

"I was his woman, I suppose," she said. "I mean, we weren't married, or anything . . . and we weren't in love . . ."

She stopped speaking, but he sensed that she wasn't finished so he remained silent.

"I think I was glad I had finally found a man

who wasn't . . . put off by my size. You're a big man, but being a *big man* is not the same as being a big woman, you know."

He didn't reply.

"A lot of men don't like big women," she went on. "Some of them would even think of me as fat."

"You're not fat," he said.

"You say that because you're a big man—"

"Any man who would take a second thought about having you is a fool, big man or small."

"Does that include you?" she asked.

There was something in her tone that gave Pike pause.

"What are you saying?"

"I'm saying that since you killed Murphy, everything that was his belongs to you, now."

"And?"

"And, I suppose, that includes me."

"Look . . . I don't know your name . . ."

"Flora."

"Flora, I don't know what you're getting at—"

"I'm getting at this," she said. Her hands went to her shirt and she didn't bother unbuttoning it. She tore it open, sending two of the buttons flying. One of them struck him in the face, but he didn't even notice. He was staring at her breasts, which were large, pear-shaped, and firm-looking. The flesh of her breasts was paler than that of her face and arms, and her nipples were dark-brown, large and wide.

"Well?" she said.

"Flora—"

"Are you going to prove yourself a fool?"

This was crazy, he thought, but he was aroused

by her — by her and the situation — and he was not going to prove himself a fool.

"No," he said, closing the gap between them, "no, I'm not."

Their lovemaking was the most violent Pike had ever experienced. For a moment he even thought she might be trying to make him pay for killing Murphy, but, when he saw her glazed eyes and the expression of pleasure on her face, he knew that wasn't the case.

Pike had not yet buttoned his shirt when he entered the tent, and when he approached her she had pulled it off him in one swift movement. He had pulled her to him then, crushing those big, firm breasts against his chest. When she moved to put her arms around his neck he could feel the muscles moving beneath her skin. She was a big woman, solidly built, and she filled his arms and hands.

They were both much too big to fit on Murphy's pallet together, so they simply sank to the floor, still locked together. They struggled with the remainder of their clothes, until they were both naked. Unclothed, there seemed to be even more of Flora, acres of her flesh for his mouth and hands to explore. He sucked her nipples while his hands roamed below, finding folds of hot, moist flesh, wherever he stroked. They were still kissing when his fingers slipped inside her.

She tore her mouth from his and moaned, "Oh, God . . ." as he held her breasts, squeezing them, thumbing the nipples. He slid his hands around her back, and then down to her big, firm buttocks. He rubbed them, one hand on each, then slid the middle finger of one hand along the crack between her cheeks. He found her anus and teased it, and she caught her breath and hugged him.

He tried to turn her over on her back to mount her, but she said, "Wait, wait . . ." and breathlessly pushed him onto his back, instead.

She kissed his chest, running her tongue over his nipples, then licked her way down the length of his body, kissing his thighs and fondling his balls with her hand. She nipped the flesh of his inner thighs, sucked it, then slowly and lasciviously worked her way toward his rigid penis.

Now she held his balls in both hands, caressing them, while she licked the head of his penis. She worked her tongue up and down his cock, wetting it so that the air felt cold against it. Suddenly, the coldness turned to heat as she took him into her mouth. She moaned as she sucked him, getting up on her knees, and closing one hand around the base of his penis. Her head bobbed up and down and he lifted his hips to meet the pull of her mouth. When he felt as if he were going to explode, he hurriedly pulled her off him. She murmured, "No," in a pleading tone, but he forcefully flipped her over onto her back and spread her legs. He leaned down between her meaty thighs and began to lick her. She reached for his head and held it, throwing her legs even wider to accommodate his insistent tongue.

He mounted her then, without giving her time to recover, and slammed into her hard. She immediately wrapped her powerful thighs around him and he slid his hands beneath her, cupping her buttocks, pulling her to him every time he thrust into her.

"God, oh God," she whispered urgently, "you're

125

. . . splitting me . . . in two . . ."

He growled and drove into her even harder.

"Don't stop," she said, "don't . . . don't . . ."

"Don't worry," he said, into her ear, "I won't."

He had no intentions of stopping, not until he had satisfied his own need, the need that had been growing inside of him for weeks. It was not so much a need for sex, as it was the need for release . . . and with a loud groan he finally had it . . .

He stood up and dressed without a word.

"When are you leaving?" she asked.

"In the morning."

"Take me with you."

He looked down at her. She was lying on her back, her big breasts flattened against her chest. Suddenly, she sat up and gazed at him, her eyes pleading. He saw her in a different light, now that she was not an object of his barely controlled, animal lust. Her hair was a mess, tangled and dirty. Her belly was soft and flabby, her thighs *too* meaty. She was a big, earthy, lusty woman, all right; but if she only lost some weight and cleaned herself up a little she would be an attractive one.

He supposed he was no bargain, either, at the moment. He was dirty and sweaty from the fight, and probably smelled like a goat. Still was too consumed by his "quest" for her kind of companionship. There was no way he could ever take her with him.

"No."

"I'll cook for you," she said, "I'll clean and darn your clothes—"

"No."

126

"I'll be your squaw!" she said, grabbing his arm. "Take me away from here!"

He pushed her away roughly. She fell onto her buttocks, her breasts and belly jiggling.

"I don't need a damned squaw!" he shouted at her.

"Please . . ." she said.

He leaned over, his hands on his knees, and spoke to her.

"Stay here," he said, "in this tent. It's yours, it and everything in it. Look around, Flora, you'll find things in here that will be of value to you."

"Please . . ." she said again, but he closed his ears to her pleas, turned, and left.

PART THREE

THREE DOWN,
TWO TO GO

CHAPTER FIFTEEN

Dan Tilson knew he had to leave Lisa's Fort.

All of a sudden, all anyone was talking about was the crew that had wiped out an entire settlement. The rumors had it that they had gotten away with a lot of money. The rumors were only half right. They *had* wiped out an entire settlement, but there had only been fifteen people in the entire place—and six of those were Indians. Why were they making such a fuss? And they hadn't exactly gotten away with a *lot* of money. As a matter of fact he was going to have to dip into his kick pretty soon, because other than the money they had stolen he had very little left.

After a month, the people at Lisa's Fort had come to accept Dan Tilson. Now that the talk was about the "Settlement Massacre" and the tone one of anger and outrage, Tilson was starting to get edgy.

It was time to leave.

Tilson rolled over and bumped into the whore.

He frowned, not remembering her for a moment. He rolled back the other way and his hand bumped into the empty whiskey bottle on the floor. That he remembered, and maybe that was why he didn't remember the whore.

He turned the blanket down so he could look at her. She was white, with brown hair, and long slender legs. In fact, she was slender all over, except for her breasts. They were huge, and it was a wonder that a slim girl like her could even stand up straight. At the moment her breasts were flattened against her chest, but when she moaned and rolled over, they sort of flopped over to one side.

Tilson stared at her a moment longer, made a face, and got to his feet. He dressed, and then used the tip of his right moccasin to wake her up.

"Wha—" she said, coming awake.

"Did I pay you?" he asked.

Still half asleep, she stared up at him, not quite comprehending what he had said. In fact, if she had been more awake, she probably would have lied to him.

"Did I pay you?" he repeated, prodding her with his foot again.

"Hey!" she said, swiping at his foot. "Yeah, yeah, you paid me."

He decided not to ask her how much, because it probably hadn't been worth it.

"Get dressed and get out," Tilson said, and stood there watching while she dressed.

"This is the last time I—"

"It sure is," he said, interrupting her, "now get your sagging tits out of here."

She looked down at her sagging tits, took a deep breath as if to hitch them up, then gave up, shrugged, and left.

After she was gone Tilson checked his kick to see if he'd dipped into it to pay her—and he had. He dropped the money back into the bag and stuffed it inside his shirt. He was going to have to use the money to get outfitted and get out of Lisa's Fort. Even though he knew they had left no witnesses, he was too jumpy to stay at the Fort any longer considering the general mood of the place.

He left the tent and headed for the trading post.

Three days later Pike, McConnell and Buck rode into Lisa's Fort. It wasn't as big a settlement as Clark's Fort, but it was getting there.

All three of them were tired, but Pike was the only one unwilling to admit it.

"I'm going to start looking for Tilson," Pike said. He dismounted and handed his horse's reins to Buck.

McConnell knew better than to argue. Besides, the Fort was larger than the camp in which they had found Mitch Murphy, and was not likely to be as closely knit.

"We'll need to reoutfit," McConnell said. "I'll set up camp and then go over to the trading post."

"Camp north of the settlement," Pike said. "I'll find you there."

McConnell nodded, and Pike walked away while his friend and Buck rode north.

Pike found the tent that served as the settlement's saloon, and went inside. It was early in the day, and the place wasn't doing much business. Pike walked up to the makeshift bar, which had been formed out of wooden planks, and ordered a whiskey. When the bartender brought it he decided to use the direct approach.

"Do you know a man named Tilson?"

"Tilson," the man said. "I might. Why?"

"I'm looking for him."

"Why?"

"Are you a friend of his," Pike asked, glowering at the man, "or are you just nosy?"

"Hey," the bartender said, putting his hands up, "I was just asking . . ."

"Yeah, well, I'm doing the asking," Pike said. "Do you know a man named Tilson, Dan Tilson."

"Yeah, I know him."

"Where is he?"

"That I don't know."

"Don't know," Pike asked, "or won't say?"

The man gave Pike a level stare and said, "I can't say because I don't know."

"When's the last time you saw him?"

"I don't know," the man said, "a few days ago, maybe."

"Maybe more?"

The man thought a moment and then said, "No, it was a few days ago — three, maybe four days, but no more."

"Three or four days," Pike repeated. "How long was he here?"

"Here?"

"At Lisa's Fort."

"Oh . . . I don't know, a few weeks, maybe a month — I don't know."

"Maybe a month . . ."

134

Pike drank his whiskey and said, "Thanks for the information."

"Listen," the bartender said as Pike was leaving, "why are you looking for him?"

Pike just stared at him. The man shrugged. "So I'm nosy."

"I'm going to kill him," Pike said.

Pike turned to leave, and thought of one last question.

"Tell me, are there any whores at this settlement?"

"Yeah," the man said, "two. You want one?"

"I want to talk to them. Where can I find them?"

"Did you just get in?"

"Yes."

"Then don't worry," the bartender said, "they'll find you."

Pike walked to the north end of the settlement and found Buck tending their horses. McConnell had set up camp, and had apparently gone to the trading post to reoutfit.

Pike clapped Buck on the back. "Take good care of those horses, boy."

"I will," Buck said with a smile. "Skins, he go to trading post."

"I figured as much."

Pike had a pot of coffee started by the time McConnell returned.

"The supplies will be ready whenever we want to pick them up."

"Good," Pike said, handing his friend a cup of coffee.

135

"What did you find out about Tilson?"

"According to the bartender, Tilson arrived here about a month ago. He hasn't seen him for three or four days, though. What does that tell you?"

"Well, he's either holed up with a woman," McConnell said, "or he's left."

"That's what I figure," Pike said. "There's two whores in town. Let's check with them before we assume he's left."

"You do that," McConnell said. "I'll go back to the trading post. If he left within the last three or four days the owner should remember outfitting him."

"All right."

"And if he's left?"

"We'll have to track him," Pike said. "Since he's the fourth one, maybe he'll lead us to number five."

"Five," McConnell repeated, thoughtfully.

"What is it?" Pike asked.

"Well, I just thought of something," McConnell said. "At the trading post I heard about something they're calling the 'settlement massacre.' "

Pike frowned. "What's that?"

"Apparently, five men wiped out a small settlement down around the Big Horn River."

"An entire settlement?" Pike shook his head in disbelief.

"Yeah," McConnell said. "They killed everyone and took what they wanted."

"Wait a minute," Pike said, "I see what you're getting at. Five men . . . maybe *our* five men.

"Right," McConnell said. "Either before or after what they did to Sun Rising, they also wiped out this little settlement. And then they split up to hide out for a while."

"My guess is they were hiding even when they found Sun Rising," Pike said. "They would see no reason to split up *and* hide because of what they did to a squaw woman."

"Agreed."

Pike looked into the distance and said, "So, it looks like I'm dispensing justice after all, and not just vengeance."

"If they're the same five."

"Yeah," Pike said, looking at McConnell, "if they are . . ."

CHAPTER SIXTEEN

Pike figured he'd find the whores — or they would find him — in the saloon that night.

He spent most of the day walking around the settlement, watching the people, watching the women work and the children play. He hadn't taken the time to just *watch* anything — women, children, animals, flowers — in a long time . . . and now that he *was* doing it, he felt guilty about it. He turned and headed for the saloon.

McConnell went back to the trading post.

"Back for your supplies so soon?" the owner asked. He had introduced himself as Adam Kyle. He was in his sixties, and ran the small trading post alone since his wife died the year before.

"No, not just yet," McConnell said. "I was wondering about a man named Tilson."

"Tilson?" Kyle said, frowning, trying to place the name. "Oh, wait, do you mean Dan Tilson?"

"That's the man," McConnell said.

"If I'm not mistaken," Kyle continued, "he came here about a month ago."

"That's what we heard."

"We?"

"My friend and me," McConnell said. He hadn't introduced himself earlier, so he did it now.

"My name is Skins McConnell. My friend is Jack Pike."

"Pike," Kyle said. "Now there's a name I know."

"Did you outfit Tilson anytime over the past three or four days?"

"I believe I did," Kyle said.

"Have you seen him since then?"

Kyle thought a moment and said, "No, I haven't."

"That doesn't necessarily mean he's gone," McConnell said, half to himself.

"He outfitted himself pretty heavily," Kyle said, "if that helps."

"It might, Mr. Kyle," McConnell said, "it might. Thanks."

McConnell found Pike in the saloon tent, staring morosely into a glass of beer.

"Anything?"

Pike looked up and McConnell could see from his eyes that it was far from his first beer. He sat opposite his friend.

"If you mean have I been approached by a whore yet, the answer is no," Pike said, still staring into his glass. "I haven't even seen a woman yet."

They had one of the few tables in the place, and Pike put his glass down on it.

"Mr. Kyle at the trading post says he remembers outfitting Tilson for a long trip."

"He can't know we're after him," Pike said. "There's no way."

"Maybe he's just hunting."

"Maybe," Pike said. "We'll talk to these whores

139

tonight, and start after him in the morning."

McConnell nodded and said, "Fine."

"Want a beer?" Pike asked.

"I'll get it," McConnell said, standing up.

"Get me another one, too."

McConnell was about to try and talk him out of it, but decided against it.

As McConnell was returning with the two beers he saw the woman enter the saloon. She was tall and slender, except for very large breasts which had begun to sag. She looked around the room and when her eyes fell on Pike, they seemed to light up. She took a deep breath, squared her shoulders in an attempt to lift her breasts, and started toward him.

When McConnell reached the table she was already sitting opposite Pike.

". . . not interested," Pike was saying, "but I want to ask you some questions."

"Talkin' or lovin'," the girl said. "It all costs the same."

McConnell sat down and took Pike's beer.

He slid his own beer in front of the girl.

"Hey, thanks," she said. She took the beer and sipped it, then looked from Pike to McConnell and back again.

"Two of you costs double."

"I told you," Pike said, "I only want to talk."

She sipped some more beer and smiled with foam on her upper lip. McConnell thought she looked kind of cute like that, and wondered what she would charge to let him lick it off.

"There's still two of you," she said.

"I'll be the only one talking."

"What will he be doin'?" she asked, looking at

140

McConnell.

"He'll just be looking."

McConnell smiled at her.

"One dollar for lookin'," she said to him, and McConnell magnanimously took out a dollar and gave it to her.

"Thanks." She tucked it away beneath her shawl, giving them both a flash of her upper breasts in the process. She looked at Pike and said, "What do you want to talk about?"

"Don't you want to discuss price, first?"

She smiled at Pike and said, "You have a face I can trust. You'll treat me fair."

"You made me give you a dollar," McConnell said, indignantly.

She graced him with a smile and said, "No offense intended."

McConnell guessed that she was about twenty-five and after being on the move so long, she might be worth whatever her price was. She might have had unfortunately oversized breasts, but she had personality.

"So," she said to Pike, "ask away."

"Do you know a man named Dan Tilson?"

Suddenly, her good humor faded.

"That bastard?"

"I guess you know him, then."

"We done some business," she said. "He ain't much of a gentleman."

"Do you know where I can find him?"

"No."

"Where did you do business?"

"In his tent," she said. "He had a tent pitched near the leanto at the south end."

"That where he kept his animals?"

141

"I guess."

"When was the last time you did business with him?"

"Oh, three, four days ago."

"And you haven't seen him since?"

"Ain't seen him and don't want to."

"I understand there's another, uh, lady who does your kind of business."

"April," she said, nodding, "only she didn't do business with him."

"You know that for a fact?"

"Yup."

"Okay," Pike said, "one last thing. What's Tilson look like?"

She frowned and said, "You're lookin' for him and you don't know what he looks like?"

"That's why I'm asking you."

She shrugged and said, "Well, he's about as tall as your silent partner here, dark hair, brown eyes, thirty-eight or so, maybe forty. Looks thirty-eight on a good day."

"What's your name?"

"Kathy."

"Well, Kathy," Pike said, taking out some money and putting it on the table, "I hope this covers your time."

She looked at the money, then put her hand over it and pulled it to her side of the table.

"That covers it," she said.

"Thanks for your help."

"Sure," she said. "By the way, what's your name?"

"Pike," he said. "This is my friend, Skins."

"Well," she said, picking the money up, "I hope you find what you're looking for."

"Don't worry," he said, "I will."

He stood up and she said, "Are you sure there ain't something else I can do for you?"

"No, Kathy," he said, "not tonight, but maybe my friend here has some other ideas."

Pike winked at McConnell and left.

Kathy looked at McConnell expectantly and said, "Well, what about it, honey? You been staring at them all this time. I know they sag a bit, but you wanna find out if they're real?"

"To tell you the truth, Kathy," McConnell said, "I wouldn't mind a bit."

McConnell didn't want to take her back to the camp. Not with Buck there. Fortunately she knew a place where they could go to be alone.

She took him to a small tent out behind the trading post that looked barely large enough to accommodate two people sitting still, let alone doing what they were going to be doing in a matter of minutes.

"Just wait here," she said. "April and I share this tent. I just have to make sure she's not in there with someone."

It seemed to McConnell that if there were two people in that tent, they would know it. Still, he waited while she trotted ahead to check.

When she came running back, he watched her bouncing breasts with fascination.

"It's all right," she said, taking his arm. "It's empty."

"Let's go," he said.

She pressed one breast against his arm and they walked to the tent.

143

"Where is Skins?" Buck asked.

"He's busy," Pike said.

"Busy?" Buck said. "Doing what?"

"Never mind," Pike said, handing Buck a plate of beans. "Just eat."

"Skins is missing dinner," the Crow boy said around a mouthful of beans.

"Believe me," Pike said, "he won't mind."

They did sag a bit, but McConnell was surprised to find them firm to the touch.

He watched as she undressed, unveiling those oversized breasts slowly, like someone unwrapping a Christmas present. They were pear-shaped and pale, with huge, brown nipples.

"Get undressed," she told him, "and sit cross-legged on the blanket."

When he did as she asked, she knelt down in front of him, and lifted her breasts toward him. "Go ahead. Touch them."

He reached out and palmed them, taking their weight in his hands.

"They're a lot firmer than they look, huh?"

"Let me ask you something," McConnell said.

"What?"

He popped her nipples with his thumbs and asked, "Do you like having tits this big?"

"Well, honey," she said, "the good Lord give them to me, and I ain't exactly ashamed of them."

He took her by the shoulders and pulled her to him so he could kiss the slopes of her breasts, and take her nipples into his mouth. She reached down and encircled his engorged cock with her hands as

144

it rose up from his lap.

"Let me ask you something," she whispered.

"What?"

She closed her hand over him and held him tightly.

"Do you like having a dick this big?"

Before he could answer, she lowered her head and slid him into her mouth. She sucked on him noisily, wetting him thoroughly, then released him. The air on his wet dick felt cold, but she fixed that almost immediately. She hiked herself into his lap and sat on him, engulfing him with her slick, hot pussy.

"Jesus . . ." he said.

She put her arms on his shoulders and he sucked her nipples while she proceeded to ride him all the way home.

CHAPTER SEVENTEEN

"Hello?"

The voice was that of a woman, and Pike was surprised enough to hesitate before answering.

"Hello?" she called again.

"Come ahead," Pike finally said.

He watched as she walked in from the darkness, coming from the direction of the settlement. He couldn't see her face, but she had a shapely form and moved like a young woman. When she came within the circle of light from the campfire he saw that she was young, about twenty-three or so, and she was pretty.

Pike looked over at Buck and could tell that he thought the girl was pretty, too. He was staring at her, not having seen many blondes in his short lifetime.

"Hello," she said to Pike, then looked at Buck and said, "Hi, there."

Buck smiled at her.

"Can I do something for you?" Pike asked.

"I don't know," she said. "That coffee smells pretty nice."

146

"Sit, and have some," Pike invited. She sat opposite him and he poured her a cup.

She was wearing a plain skirt and shirt, and had a shawl wrapped around her shoulders. Her hands, when she accepted the cup, were smooth and strong looking. Strong as they may have been, though, they didn't look as if she had done any hard work recently — not *physical* work, anyway.

"It's good," she said, after a sip.

"It's awful," he said. "My partner usually makes it, but he's uh, busy tonight."

"I know," she said. "I saw him with Kathy."

"You know Kathy?"

"Sure," she said. "We're in the same line of work."

"Oh," Pike said, surprised. "You're . . ."

"A whore," she said. "Yes."

"No," Pike said, "I was going to say, you're April."

"That's right," she said, "but I'm not ashamed to be called a whore. Whoring is honest work."

"Sure it is," Pike said. "It's about as honest as you can get."

"Yes," she said, cocking her head to one side and looking at him, appraising him, "it is, isn't it?"

He poured himself a cup of coffee, then remembered Buck. He looked at the boy, who was just sitting there, staring at April.

"Time for bed, boy."

Buck continued to stare at April, and Pike leaned over and nudged him.

"What?"

"I said time for bed, Buck."

"But Pike—"

"Git."

The boy frowned, stood up and took one last, furtive look at the blonde woman.

"Good-night, Buck," she said, and that seemed to delight him so much that he went off to bed immediately with a big grin on his face.

"Is he yours?" she asked.

"No," Pike said, "he's just travelling with us."

"I see."

There was an awkward silence between them, and Pike decided to break it.

"Are you here about Tilson?"

She sipped her coffee, "I didn't know the man. Kathy must have told you that. He was her customer."

"Yes, she did," Pike said. "Why are you here, then? Are you, uh, looking for . . ."

"Work?" she asked, smiling. "Well, I wouldn't mind it, if you'd like, but that's not why I'm here."

"Why are you here, then?"

"I want to hire you."

"As what?"

"Whatever you want to call it," she said. "Guide, chaperone, bodyguard. I want to get out of here."

"And you want me to take you?"

"That's right."

"I'm sorry, but I've got something to do—"

"Oh, I wouldn't interfere," she said. "You can just drop me at the next settlement we come to."

"I'm sorry—"

"There's a reason you should take me," she said, "other than money, I mean."

"If you mean your services along the way—"

"No," she said, "I don't mean that. You see, Kathy talked to me about Tilson."

"Is there something she didn't tell us?"

"Well, not deliberately," she said. "You see,

Kathy's not the smartest girl in the world."

"What are you getting at?" Pike asked.

"Tilson talked to Kathy about his friends," she said. "You know, pillow talk."

"Did he name names?"

"He did."

"And?"

"I can give them to you."

"Look, lady, maybe you should know that when I find Tilson I aim to kill him—him and his . . . friends."

"From the look of you," she said, "I'd say you'd probably killed some of them already."

"Why don't you give me the names, and then we'll see if we can do business."

"All right," she said. "There's Haywood . . ."

"Go on."

"Murphy . . . Hecox . . ."

"Keep going."

"You got them already, huh?"

Between his teeth he said, "Don't drag this out."

"Raitt," she said, "Bert Raitt."

"Bert Raitt."

"Do you know him?"

"No," he said, "but he'll know me. Thanks for his name."

"Is Raitt the last?"

"Yes."

She was quiet for a moment, as she realized that what Pike meant was that he'd already killed three of the men.

"When are you leaving?" she asked quietly.

"Tomorrow morning."

"Are you taking me with you?"

"No."

149

"I didn't think so," she said. "Could I have some more coffee?"

"Look—"

"I know where Raitt is," she said.

He stared at her, picked up the coffee pot and refilled her cup.

"You see," she said, over the rim of the fresh cup, "I know Bert Raitt. I happen know that he has a wife at Pierre's Hole."

"Pierre's Hole."

"He was the leader," he said, "Tilson's and the others. Whatever they did to you, he was the leader when they did it."

She drank her coffee and let him digest what she had told him.

"Look," she said, breaking the silence, "I didn't have to tell you about Pierre's Hole. I could have held it back and made you take me with you, but I decided to play it straight with you. Now I expect you to play it the same way with me."

Pike poured himself a fresh cup of coffee. She was right, she had helped him out, and although she had her own motives, she deserved his thanks.

"You be ready to travel at first light," he said.

"I'll be here," she said. "I have a horse, I can get supplies—"

"We have supplies," Pike said. "Just be here with your horse, ready to ride."

"Of course," she said, after a moment, "I could stay—"

"No, thanks," Pike said. "No offense . . . but no."

She shrugged and said, "Whatever you say," handing the cup back to him. "You're the boss."

"Remember that," he said.

She smiled at him and said, "I will. Thanks, Mr.

150

Pike."

"Just Pike," he said.

"Pike," she said. "The name's April Dancer."

"See you in the morning, April Dancer."

She stood there a moment longer, maybe expecting him to change his mind, and then melted away into the darkness.

Pike sat there, thinking about Dan Tilson and Bert Raitt. In the morning, they would take off after Tilson, try to pick up his trail. With luck, he'd be on his way to Pierre's Hole. If his trail deviated, then they'd head straight for the Hole. Sooner or later, Tilson would show up, especially when he couldn't find any of his other friends.

Pike would just as soon head straight for the Hole, and Bert Raitt . . . the leader of the pack.

Pike woke up when McConnell entered the tent. Buck was lying on his side with his back to them, asleep.

"So?" Pike asked.

"So what?"

"Did you find out anything else about Tilson?"

McConnell squirmed under his blanket. "To tell you the truth, we didn't talk much."

Pike laid back. "Now why doesn't that surprise me?"

"We leavin' in the mornin'?" McConnell asked.

"First light," Pike said, "and we got company."

"Who?"

"Gal name of April."

"The other whore?"

"That's right."

"Why are we takin' her?"

"Because I spent some time with her," Pike said, "and all *we* did was talk . . ."

Dan Tilson didn't know for sure where Bert Raitt was holed up, but he thought he had a pretty good idea where the man would go. None of the others knew it, but Raitt was married. Sure, he didn't act like a married man, whorin' whenever he got the chance, but he'd been married for the past five years to a white woman who waited for him at Pierre's Hole, near where the Big Horn River met the South Pass. It was about three days ride, but he figured to do some hunting along the way. He was pretty sure that Raitt was going to be mad when he showed up at the Hole, but Tilson just didn't know where else to light.

Raitt was their leader, wasn't he? And right about now, Dan Tilson needed to be led.

CHAPTER EIGHTEEN

The next morning, when Pike and McConnell came out of their tent, they found coffee already on the fire and April Dancer seated there, waiting for them.

"I figured we'd travel a little better with some coffee in our bellies."

Today she was wearing pants, a shirt, and a jacket, and a pair of boots. She poured two cups of coffee and handed one to both Pike and McConnell.

"Hi, I'm April," she said as she handed Skins his cup.

"Skins McConnell," McConnell said. "Just call me Skins."

"Where's Buck? Should we make him some breakfast?" she asked.

At that moment Buck came out of the tent.

"Buck, go get the horses," Pike said. He turned to April and said, "He can wait until later to eat."

"Are we takin' the tent with us?" McConnell asked Pike.

"No," Pike said, "I don't want to take the time to pack it. April, dump the rest of that coffee and kill the fire."

"I'll go to the trading post and pick up our supplies," McConnell said.

"You'll have to wake Mr. Kyle," April said.

"I'll wake him," McConnell said. "I'll meet you back here."

He went to get one of the mules and walked with it to the trading post.

April doused the fire with the remainder of the coffee, then kicked the ashes. Her horse was nearby, a good-looking mountain pony.

"Where did you get the horse?" Pike asked.

"I bought it," she said. "I've saved my money. That reminds me, we didn't discuss a price."

"No price," Pike said. "This is my way of saying thanks."

She smiled at him. "That's nice."

"Yeah," Pike grunted. Now that morning had come he wasn't happy that he had agreed to take her along, but he was a man of his word, and would not change his mind.

Buck came over with the animals, all but the mule McConnell had walked over to the trading post. The Crow boy stood there, holding the animal's reins, and staring at April.

"Do you have a gun?" Pike asked April.

"A gun? Why would I have a gun?"

"Do you know how to use a gun?"

"I've never had to," she said. "My customers are usually satisfied. Will I need a gun on this trip?"

"Probably not," Pike said. "I just wanted to know."

"Maybe along the way you could teach me how to use one," April suggested, "just in case."

"Yeah," Pike said, "maybe."

"Look, Pike," April said, "I know you're not

154

happy about my coming along, but I'll earn my keep. I'll work, and I can cook."

At that moment McConnell returned with the mule and he and Pike set about splitting the load with their other mules. When the supplies were evenly distributed, they all mounted up.

"I'm going to ride back here with Buck," April announced, moving her horse alongside of the Crow boy's animal. "Is that all right with you, Buck?"

Buck stared at her, his eyes wide, and said, "Yes."

"You two don't have to worry about us," she announced, putting her hand on Buck's shoulder, "we can take care of each other."

"What does she mean by that?" McConnell asked Pike, looking anxious as they started their trip.

Pike frowned at his friend, then realized why he was so worried, and smiled.

"Don't worry, Skins," he said. "Buck is too young for her."

"Who knows?" McConnell said. "If he was back with his own people, he'd almost be considered a man. A young warrior."

"Stop playing the worried daddy," Pike said. "We've got other things to worry about."

"Like what?"

"Like Bert Raitt. Do you know him?"

"I never heard of him."

"Neither have I."

"Are we gonna go for Tilson, or Raitt."

Pike told McConnell what he had figured, about following Tilson's trail as long as it led to Pierre's Hole.

"So if the trail breaks off, we'll keep going to the Hole for this Raitt fella?"

"That's right," Pike said. "At least we have some

155

idea of where he is. Once we get him, we can either wait for Tilson, or start hunting him. He'll be the last at that point, and we could take our time running him down."

"No matter how long it took."

"That's right," Pike said, "no matter how long."

"Pike . . ." McConnell said, then stopped.

"What is it?"

"Well, I want to ask you something, but I don't want you gettin' mad at me."

"Go ahead and ask."

"What's gonna happen when they're all dead?"

"What do you mean?"

"I mean, what will you do, then? Go back to the way it was before?"

"It can't be the way it was before. Sun Rising is gone."

"Well then, back to the way it was before Sun Rising came into your life."

"I don't know, Skins," Pike said. "I don't know how I'm going to feel when this is all over. I don't know what kind of man I'll be by then."

"Well, maybe you can make sure what kind of man you'll be by stopping now."

"Stopping?"

"Just quitting this."

"And let them go?" Pike asked. "Let the last two of them live?"

"Yes," McConnell said, knowing full well that Pike just wouldn't — or couldn't — do that. Still, he had felt the need to bring it up.

"If I do that," Pike said, "then the blood of anyone they killed from here on out would be on my hands, Skins. I wouldn't want that . . . would you?"

"No," McConnell said, "no, Pike, I sure

156

wouldn't."

They both fell silent. As they rode away from Lisa's Fort, they started to scan the ground for signs.

McConnell had asked Mr. Kyle at the trading post if he'd outfitted anyone else between Tilson and now, and the man had not. Whatever tracks led out of the Fort might be three or four days old, but they'd be Tilson's. At least they'd start out in the right direction. Once they got far enough away from the Fort and started finding cold campsites, it would be anyone's guess whether or not they were Tilson's. As long as the cold trail pointed the way toward Pierre's Hole, though, they'd just keep following it.

Tilson had a decision to make.

He was at a point where he could either continue on to Pierre's Hole, or veer off and start in another direction. There were other places he could go, but there'd be people there too, and the word of the settlement massacre had no doubt spread. It was the nature of the mountains, even with the miles that separated settlements and camps, that news of what he and his partners had done would always catch up to him, no matter how far he ran. Now he was forced to make an important decision on his own, which was not something he was used to doing.

In the end the decision was ultimately made for him by Raitt. Tilson knew how angry Raitt would be if he were to ride into Pierre's Hole bold as brass, and Tilson didn't want to face an angry Bert Raitt.

He wondered how Raitt would deal with the news that was about to reach Pierre's Hole.

157

PART FOUR

PIERRE'S HOLE

CHAPTER NINETEEN

Bert Raitt rolled over in bed and looked at his wife, Rae, lying next to him. They had joked about her name when they were planning to get married. Bert thought it sounded funny, "Rae Raitt." She, on the other hand, had thought it sounded wonderful.

She was still fast asleep, and he sat up, and stared at her. She had long dark hair, which had fanned out on the pillow behind her head. She was not beautiful, but she was very pretty. Her eyes were closed but when they were open they were the clearest blue he had ever seen. She was not tall, and her body was full in the hips and breasts, which sometimes made her appear even shorter than she was. Those breasts and hips, though, were just perfect for lovemaking, and Raitt loved lying on top of her.

He wondered idly why he liked to rape other women when he had Rae waiting for him here in Pierre's Hole?

Of course, she knew nothing about the women he had raped, or the men and women he had killed. Here in Pierre's Hole, which was a growing mountain community, Bert Raitt was looked upon as a good neighbor and a hard worker. He had worked very

161

hard building the two room cabin that he and Rae shared, and he had also worked hard helping several of his neighbors build their cabins, as well.

In Pierre's Hole, Bert Raitt was considered a good man, a concerned citizen, a loving husband and — he laid his hand over Rae's belly, which was distended with child — soon a loving father, as well.

Outside of Pierre's Hole, however, he was a thief, a rapist, and a cold-blooded murderer.

Whenever he felt those urges coming over him — well, that's when he'd tell Rae that he was going hunting. Only she had no idea what he was hunting for.

What would she do, he wondered, if she did find out?

Just recently the news of the "settlement massacre" had reached Pierre's Hole, and the people had reacted with shocked outrage — including Bert Raitt. How, he heard himself ask his neighbors, could someone do such a thing? Maybe, he had suggested, they should set up some security, maybe even elect a lawman and some deputies, just to make sure that the same thing never happened here in Pierre's Hole.

Raitt swung his feet to the floor. He often wondered what his neighbors would think if he and his boys decided to rob Pierre's Hole and burn it to the ground. Of course, they'd have to kill everyone, and there were a few women he wouldn't mind raping — Glenn Boyd's wife, for one. She was older than Rae, but even at forty, Laura Boyd was an earthy beauty with a solid body — not unlike Rae's, only Laura Boyd was a lot taller. And then there was Leanne Kent, Jesse Kent's wife. Leanne was barely twenty and had the blondest hair Raitt had ever seen. When the sun was high, the down on her arms almost glowed and

162

once, when she'd had her hair piled high on her head, he'd seen the down on the back of her neck glow, as well. He wondered if the hair between her legs was as golden blonde as the hair on her head. She was tall, and small breasted, although she carried those breasts high and proud. Raitt bet they weren't much bigger than peaches, and probably as hard.

He stood up and reached for his pants. He didn't guess he'd be raping Laura Boyd or Leanne Kent anytime soon. Pierre's Hole was too valuable to him as a hiding place. After every one of his robberies he would always return here, where he was known as good ol' Bert Raitt. He had always warned his men — Murphy, Haywood, Tilson, and all the others he'd used over the past few years — never to come to Pierre's Hole. In fact, only Tilson and Murphy knew about his life in the Hole. He'd never even told any of the others he was married, let alone where he lived. Fact was, he didn't even know why he'd told Tilson and Murphy, but they'd all three been drunk at the time and it had just come tumbling out. He'd sworn them both to secrecy and so far neither of them had ever spoken a word.

If they ever did — or if either of them ever actually showed up — he'd kill them, and they knew it.

He pulled on his pants and looked around for a shirt. While he was putting it on, Rae reached over to his side of the bed, and when she didn't find him there she opened her eyes.

"Bert?"

"Go back to sleep, honey."

She rubbed her eyes and asked, "What are you doing up so early?"

"I promised Jesse I'd help him fix that leaky wall in his cabin," he said. "I want to get an early start."

"You're always helping somebody Bert," she said, with admiration.

"I know, honey," he said. "They're my neighbors, what else can I do?"

"Come here and kiss me," she said, "that's what you can do."

She lifted her arms to him, at the same time lifting those fine, firm breasts. He went to her, kissed the nipple of each breast, and then her mouth, while laying his hand on her swollen belly.

"One more month," she said, placing her hand over his. "I can hardly wait."

"Neither can I, honey."

"I know it's a girl."

"Just like I know it's a boy."

She laughed and said, "I guess we'll just have to wait and see who's right — ooh, did you feel that? The baby kicked."

"I felt it," he said, rubbing her belly.

"Shall I get up and make breakfast?"

"No," he said, "Jesse said that Leanne would have something waiting."

"She's beautiful, ain't she?"

"Who?"

"Leanne, silly."

"I hadn't noticed."

"Come on," she said. "She's so young, and thin, and she has a face like an angel."

"You're the only angel I'm interested in, and she ain't so much younger than you."

"Eight years," she said.

"She's still a girl," he said, "and you're a woman."

"Telling a woman she's not a girl anymore is telling her she's getting old."

He stood up and said, "I'm gonna leave before I

get myself in a heap of trouble."

"You better."

He started for the door and she called, "Bert?"

"Yeah?"

"You better come back, too."

"I'll be back."

"Soon."

He smiled at her and promised, "Soon."

While walking to the Kent's cabin Raitt suddenly realized that he had an erection. He hadn't made love with Rae for months, now. She refused, not wanting to injure the baby, and he didn't want to force her. Now, on the way to Jesse and Leanne Kent's, knowing that he was going to be seeing Leanne fresh from her bed, he was fit to bust.

Raitt was worried. Was he getting to the point that he couldn't control himself any longer? To the point where Leanne Kent or Laura Boyd could drive him to destroy the only home he'd ever had? Once he got started, he knew he wouldn't stop until the Hole was just that—a hole in the middle of nowhere.

There were three or four men at the settlement who would be ripe for something like that. Raitt had a knack for finding the right kind of men—the kind who would willingly be led into rape and murder. The kind of men like Murphy, and Tilson, who would do whatever he told them to do. Generally, they were unattached men, men who were full of themselves, men who didn't have much to call their own, men who spent most of their time sitting around, drinking, and trading stories.

There were men like that everywhere, men who although they may never have killed before, or raped a

165

woman before, would willingly take part in the new experience, and revel in it, once they were led to it.

And Bert Raitt was the one who could lead them.

Leanne Kent did not like Bert Raitt.

Leanne saw something in Raitt that others at the settlement just didn't seem to see. Even her own Jesse thought Bert Raitt was the salt of the earth. Jesse, however, had never felt Bert Raitt's eyes on him the way she did, undressing her. She liked Rae Raitt well enough, but she never visited Rae when Bert was around, he scared her that much.

She was preparing breakfast for Jesse, and for Bert Raitt, because Jesse had asked her to. Bert was coming over to help Jesse fix a leaky wall, but she intended to leave as soon as the men had finished breakfast and started work. She did not want to be around Bert Raitt, not even in her own house.

She would never tell Jesse any of this; he would think she was just being foolish. But she had to talk to someone, so she decided to go see Laura Boyd. Laura was older and wiser, and maybe she would be able to tell Leanne what to do.

"There it is," Pike said, "Pierre's Hole."

"It sure has grown," McConnell said.

"Well, we haven't been here in a long time, Skins," Pike said, "I wonder if there's even anyone left that we'll know."

"Only one way to find out," McConnell said.

Pike turned and looked behind him at April and Buck. The two had become good friends during their journey to Pierre's Hole and, truth be told, he had come to like April very much, himself. She was out-going and friendly, and her open, honest nature somehow made him feel guilty about the rage he still carried inside of him. She looked at him now and smiled broadly, and he nearly smiled back at her, in spite of himself.

"Let's get movin'," McConnell said. "I've got an urge for a warm lunch."

Pike turned back and looked at his friend.

"That sounds good to me, Skins," Pike said. "A warm lunch, and then we'll find Bert Raitt."

McConnell made a face and said, "You really know how to ruin a man's appetite."

CHAPTER TWENTY

Laura Boyd took Leanne Kent's hands in hers. Leanne's hands were soft, while Laura's were rough from a lifetime of work. Soon, Leanne's hands would grow just as rough, Laura thought sadly, but for now she marveled at her young friend's beautiful, soft, long-fingered hands.

"He's the same with me," she said.

"With you?"

Leanne's obvious surprise made Laura smile.

"Is that so surprising?" she asked. "I know I'm twice your age, but believe it or not, there are still some men who still find me attractive."

"I'm sorry," Leanne said, haltingly, "I didn't mean—I mean, I know you're lovely, I just—"

"You just thought I was too old."

"Not at all!" Leanne said. "I only meant—"

"Never mind, dear," Laura said, rubbing the girl's hands, "just believe me when I say I know what you mean. I don't like Bert Raitt, either."

Leanne looked relieved.

"I thought it was just me."

"Well, it's not," Laura said. "It might just be you and

168

me, but it's not just you."

"The way he looks at me—"

"I know," Laura said, "he looks at me like I'm a piece of meat and he hasn't eaten in weeks."

"That's exactly it!" she said, "I could never put it into words, but that's it!"

"And him with a lovely wife, too," Laura said. "Rae Raitt is so sweet, I don't know how she let that man fool her the way he has."

"Do you know something—"

"Oh no," Laura said, "I don't know anything for sure about Bert Raitt, but I know men, honey, and that one is about as sincere as a snake. Oh, I know he goes around smiling, and helping people, and he's got a lot of friends hereabouts, but take my word, that man is not right in the head."

"You mean . . . he's crazy?"

"I don't know what I mean," Laura said. "Glenn says I'm imaginin' things—"

"You told your husband how you feel?"

"Of course," Laura said. "When you been married to your man as long as I been married to mine, you will too."

"And what did he say?"

"Just that, that I was imaginin' things, and that Bert Raitt was one of the finest men here at the Hole."

"That's the way most people feel."

"That's the way most men feel," Laura corrected her. "You and I know better."

"I don't know what to do, Laura," Leanne said. "Jesse likes him so much, he invites him to the house. I can't stand the way he looks at me."

"Well, unless you want your man dead, you best keep it to yourself."

"Dead? What do you mean?"

169

"I mean that if you told Jesse about this, he might go after Bert Raitt. Your Jesse is a fine young man, Leanne, but he's no match for an animal like Bert Raitt."

"Animal?"

"My guess is, Bert Raitt is a whole different man when he goes on those huntin' trips of his."

"Shouldn't we tell Rae? Warn her, I mean?"

"Oh, honey," Laura said, "what if I came to you and warned you about your husband?"

"Why, I'd say you were crazy . . ."

"Exactly," Laura said. "That's what Rae Raitt would say, as well."

Leanne let go of Laura's hands and hugged her arms, as if she were cold.

"I don't know how long I can take it, Laura."

"It shouldn't be for much longer," Laura said.

"What do you mean?"

"A rattlesnake can't hide his rattle forever, Leanne," Laura said. "Sooner or later, the real Bert Raitt will come out, and then everyone will know what he really is."

"And what will happen then?"

Laura looked at the sky, "God only knows . . ."

After she saw Leanne off Laura went back inside her cabin. She was forty years old, far from old, and yet she felt old. Oh, she knew she was still attractive — Bert Raitt never let her forget that — but sometimes she felt like an old hag. She liked Leanne Kent, but the girl was so young, so naive, so fresh, that being with her made Laura feel ancient.

What she would have liked to do right then was grab her man and take him to bed, but the time she and

170

Glenn shared in bed these days was usually spent asleep.

God help her, but once or twice when she knew Bert Raitt was watching her, she'd felt like challenging him. Either turn his eyes away or do something about what he was thinking. She dreamed once that she grabbed Raitt, pulled him into the brush, and rode him hard. She had awakened in a sweat and Glenn had asked her if she were all right, because she was flushed and trembling. It had been so long since Glenn saw her like *that* that he didn't even know what had happened. She'd felt ashamed at first, but there was still a delicious tingle between her legs, and she hadn't felt it in such a long time . . .

Of course, it wasn't really Glenn's fault. He was older than she was, sixteen years older. At fifty-six, Glenn Boyd had little interest in sex anymore. He simply ran his trading post from dawn to dusk, came home for dinner, sat outside for an hour or so, and then went to bed.

Laura loved him, but she *was* only forty years old, and she needed some lovin' badly, before she actually did grab Bert Raitt and drag him in the brush . . .

The very thought made her shiver. That she could ever have sex with a man like Bert Raitt was . . . perverse!

Maybe that was exactly why the thought had occurred to her from time to time . . .

Pike, McConnell, Buck and April rode into Pierre's Hole just after noon. There was a tent here and there, but most of the structures they saw were wood — some houses, and the others business establishments. There was a trading post, a livery — although a small one —

171

and there was even an honest to God restaurant.

"I ain't set in an honest to God restaurant since you drug me to St. Louis," McConnell said.

"Let's not even talk about that," Pike said, and McConnell agreed. In St. Louis, McConnell had been arrested for a murder he hadn't committed, and it took Pike and some good friends all they could do to absolve him.

"What is a restaurant?" Buck asked.

"A place to eat," April said. "You don't think they'd actually have a hotel, do you?" she asked Pike and McConnell hopefully. "With a bathtub?"

"Why don't we leave the animals here and have a look on foot," Pike suggested.

They dismounted and found a man inside the small livery who took their animals from them.

"Don't get many strangers around here," the man said.

"Your settlement seems to be growing," Pike said.

"Yeah. Pretty soon we'll have us a whole town. Maybe we'll get more strangers then."

"Maybe," Pike said. "Would you have a hotel hereabouts? Or something like it?"

"Somethin' like it," the man said. "Go down the street and on the right you'll see a building with a sign above the door that says 'Mabel's.' She'll have a room or two. Ain't no hotel, but it's a place to sleep."

"Does she have a bathtub?" April asked.

"I think she does."

"Well," April said, "that's where I'm headed."

"Don't you want to eat?" McConnell asked.

"I want a hot bath—or even a cold one—and some fresh clothes, and then I'll think about eating."

"Suit yourself," Pike said.

She started off, then turned and faced them.

"Thanks very much for bringing me, Pike," she said, then looked at McConnell and Buck and said, "and for the company."

"You're welcome," McConnell said. "Havin' a woman along was kinda nice—especially one who could cook."

April reached down and tousled Buck's hair.

"If you're still eating when I get done, I'll see you there."

Pike nodded, and she started off in search of her bath.

They had followed a cold trail for days, not knowing for sure whether or not it was Tilson's, but deciding to accept it as his anyway. About a day's ride from the Hole the man had apparently camped over night, and then had suddenly changed direction away from Pierre's Hole. At that point they stuck with Pike's original plan, and continued on to the settlement.

Dan Tilson would be left for another day.

Bert Raitt was now the target.

Pike, McConnell and Buck entered the restaurant. It was a small place, with only four tables and, at the moment, it was empty.

A man stepped out of a doorway in the back, a tall, bulky man wearing a white apron. He had obviously heard them enter, and had a big smile plastered across his face. When he spotted Buck, however, the smile faded.

"Can I help you fellas?" he asked.

"We'd like something to eat," Pike said.

"Yeah," McConnell said, "something hot."

173

"I'll be glad to fix you two something . . ." the man said.

"Great!" McConnell said.

". . . but I ain't feedin' him," the man added, pointing at Buck.

"What's wrong with him?" Pike asked.

The man looked at Pike as if Pike must be joking. "He's an Indian."

"He's just a boy," McConnell said.

"He's an Indian all the same," the man said, "and I ain't servin' him."

"But you'll serve us?" McConnell asked.

"Sure," the man said. "You ain't Indians."

"Well then, fine," McConnell said, "you feed me, and I'll feed him."

"What? From where?"

"From my plate."

"Oh no," the man said, "not from one of my plates."

"Skins—" Pike said, but McConnell wasn't listening.

"Listen, friend," McConnell said, "you said you'd feed us, so we'll have a couple of steaks and some vegetables—if you've got them."

"I've got them."

"Then cook them up," McConnell said, "and what I do with mine is my business."

The man stood there a moment, matching stares with McConnell, then turned around and walked away.

"Hey!" Pike called.

The man turned.

Pike held up two fingers and said, "I'll have two steaks. I'm real hungry."

The man looked at Pike and McConnell, then said, "Comin' up," and went through the back door.

McConnell turned to Pike and said, "Thanks."

"It wasn't smart to push, Skins," Pike said.

"Really?" McConnell said. "Hell, I thought I was takin' a page out of your book."

McConnell put his hand on Buck's shoulder and steered him to a table. Pike stared after his friend for a few moments, letting what McConnell said sink in, and then followed.

CHAPTER TWENTY-ONE

When the food came Pike gave one of his steaks to Buck without waiting for the owner to leave the table. The man glared, but did not have the nerve to say anything. Defiantly, he turned and went back to the kitchen.

Other customers started drifting in, and every time the owner took an order he'd whisper something to them and then they'd all look in Pike and McConnell's direction.

Soon, the place was full. Each of the four tables had people sitting at them. Nine people in all. And every one of them was staring at Buck.

"I've had enough," McConnell said, throwing down his napkin.

"Skins—"

McConnell held his hand out to stop Pike before he could go on.

"I haven't interfered with you, have I?"

"Uh, no—"

"Then let me do this."

"Fine," Pike said, "but just let me know if you intend to take on the whole place, by yourself, okay?"

176

"What are you worried about? There are only nine of them," McConnell said, as he stood up.

"Ten, counting the owner," Pike said.

McConnell turned and faced the center of the room. "What the hell's the matter with you people anyway?"

Half of the people looked away, while the others looked at McConnell in surprise.

"Haven't you ever seen people eat before?"

McConnell was looking from table to table, daring someone to answer him.

At one table a man obliged.

"That's an Indian," the man said.

"That?" McConnell said, pointing to Buck.

"That's right."

"That's a boy, Mister," McConnell said. "You want to take it out on a boy for something some Indians may have done to you?"

"The Indians never did nothin' to me," the man said.

"Then why don't you shut your big mouth?" McConnell said.

"What?"

"You heard me," McConnell said. "If you've never had trouble with Indians, you got nothin' to say."

"Hey," the man said, standing up.

McConnell moved to the middle of the room.

"We're just passing through," McConnell said. "You got a problem with us takin' a meal?"

"I got a problem with you bringing an Indian here."

The other man was bigger than McConnell, but Pike gave McConnell the edge because of his anger.

"The boy stays for as long as I stay," McConnell said, clearly challenging the man.

He was sitting with two friends, and both of them now stood up.

"You're a little outnumbered, friend, don't you

177

think?" the man asked McConnell.

"I don't think so," McConnell said. His back was to Pike, but two things told him that the big man had stood up. He heard the scrape of the chair on the floor, and he saw the eyes of all three men look up.

"Make a move, or get out," McConnell said.

The three men looked around for help, but the other diners were all studying their plates.

"We ain't ate yet," the man said, belligerently.

"Eat somewhere else."

The three men stood their ground for a few moments, but when Pike moved forward they turned toward the door. When they reached it they stopped, as if trying to make up their minds once and for all, but in the end they stormed out of the restaurant.

"Anyone else object?" McConnell asked.

No one spoke.

"Then eat your meals and stop starin'!"

Pike and McConnell went back to their table and sat down. Buck had been busy with his steak through the whole encounter, and had never looked up.

When Leanne Kent returned to her cabin she found her husband there alone, sitting at the table having a cup of coffee.

"Is it finished?" she asked.

"The wall? Yeah, it's fixed. We won't have anymore trouble when it rains."

"Good."

"Bert was a real help," Jesse said. "In fact, if it wasn't for him the wall wouldn't even be fixed. We owe him a lot."

"Uh-huh," Leanne said, looking away, but Jesse didn't notice.

"So I invited them to dinner tonight."

"You did?" Leanne said, shocked. This time Jesse was looking away, and didn't see the look on his young wife's face.

"Yes," he said, looking up at her. "You don't mind, do you? I mean, Rae is so far along that I figured she could use a night off from cooking."

"No," Leanne said, feeling a shiver down her back at the thought of Bert Raitt coming to dinner, "no, I don't mind, Jesse."

"You like Rae, don't you?"

"Sure," she said, "I like Rae a lot."

"Good," Jesse said, standing up. "I've got to go and run some errands, but I'll be back later. All right?"

"Yes," Leanne said, "yes, all right."

Jesse kissed Leanne on the cheek and left the house. Leanne sat down in the seat he had just vacated, put her face in her hands, and cried.

Bert Raitt returned home and found Rae sleeping in the bed. He knew she tired easily these days, just a month from delivering their child. There was no doctor at Pierre's Hole, but they did have a midwife—in fact, Laura Boyd was the midwife. Thinking about Laura Boyd made Bert Raitt hard again, and he shook his head to dispel the lewd and violent images racing through his mind.

He walked to the bed and looked down at his pregnant wife and decided not to wake her. Instead, he left the cabin and went for a walk.

Raitt was aware of the restless feeling inside of him. Somehow it was all connected with his fantasies about Leanne and Laura. He had agreed to having dinner that night with the Kents because he wanted to test

179

himself. If he found himself unable to control his thoughts about Leanne Kent — even in the presence of her husband and his wife — then maybe it was time for another hunting trip.

Raitt turned and headed back for the cabin. There were three men in the Hole who Raitt felt were tailor-made for his special trips. He wanted to find them and start talking them up. The three of them, with Raitt's other four men, would be able to pull off a much bigger job than the recent "settlement massacre."

Dan Tilson was having second thoughts.

All of a sudden he felt that he *had* to go to Pierre's Hole and see Bert Raitt. Once they got together they could decide what to do about the spreading rumors of their "settlement massacre." They could also get together with the others — Haywood, Hecox and Murphy — and maybe hole up somewhere together until it all blew over.

Of course, Tilson was wrong. The last thing he should have done was to get together with Bert Raitt.

Pike left money on the table to cover their meals and they left the restaurant.

"I think we'll prepare our own meals from now on," Pike said.

"That means we'd better find a campsite," McConnell said. "Buck and I can do that."

"I'll take a look around the Hole," Pike said.

"How will you know what Bert Raitt looks like?" McConnell asked.

"I'll find April," Pike said. "She can either describe him, or walk with me."

"We'll make camp and then come looking for you."

"Maybe you'd better keep Buck in camp," Pike suggested.

McConnell agreed.

"The people in the Hole don't seem to like Indians much, do they?" he said. "I'll keep an eye on the boy."

McConnell and Buck walked toward the north end of the Hole, while Pike walked in the opposite direction.

He found April coming out of Pierre's Hole's modest hotel.

"You finished eating?" she asked.

"Yes."

"I'll have to eat alone, then. Was the food at the restaurant good?"

"It was all right. Just don't let them know you're with us."

"Why?"

Pike told April what had happened at the restaurant.

"Suddenly," April said, "I've lost my appetite."

"Skins and Buck are camping north of town," Pike said.

"I can wait," she said. "Were you looking for me?"

Pike noticed how fresh April smelled, and how clean she looked. She was remarkably pretty, and very innocent-looking for a woman in her line of work.

"I was," Pike said. "I want to take a walk around and see if I can spot Raitt. I need you to describe him again, in detail."

"I have a better idea," she said. "I can walk with you and let you know when I see him."

Pike nodded. "I thought of that, but he might recognize you."

"We don't have to walk together," she said, "just within sight of each other. If I see him, I'll signal you."

Pike thought a moment. "All right, April, but if you

181

see him you're not to approach him. Do you understand?"

"Will you . . . kill him right away?"

"No," Pike said, "not right away."

"But you will kill him?"

"Eventually."

April shivered, suddenly feeling cold. "I suppose we ought to get started, then."

"Yes," Pike said. "You walk on the left side, I'll walk just behind you on the right. If you see him, put your hands on your hips."

"All right."

Pike watched her walk to the other side of the "street," a muddy strip that ran down the center of the Hole. She had become another pawn in his quest, like McConnell, like the boy.

Pike was rapidly becoming a person he did not like — and might not ever like again.

CHAPTER TWENTY-TWO

In the center of Pierre's Hole a large wooden structure had been erected. It was the largest building in the Hole, and it was the saloon. This was where Bert Raitt went to look for his three new disciples.

Matt Kincaid, Johnny Newman and Bo Peters were sitting in the saloon when Raitt entered.

"Hey, Bert," Kincaid called out. "Come and have a drink with us."

They didn't have to ask twice.

"What have you fellas been up to?" Raitt asked when he had a beer in front of him.

"Nothin' much," Kincaid said. "Just sittin' around, playin' some cards. Want to play poker?"

"No," Raitt said. "I have other things in mind to do for . . . entertainment."

"Like what?" Bo Peters asked.

"Well, it would mean leaving Pierre's Hole for a while."

"Hey," Johnny Newman, "we been out of the Hole."

"Doing what?" Raitt asked.

Newman shrugged, and looked at the other men, who also shrugged.

"I can see you fellas need a little guidance."

"What kind of guidance?" Kincaid asked.

"Some lessons on what to do with your time."

"What should we be doin' with our time?" Johnny Newman asked.

Raitt saw that he had their attention. He leaned forward and spoke to all of them.

"Well for one thing, I can help you make your time more profitable . . ."

Raitt was more than satisfied with the results of his talk with Kincaid, Newman, and Peters. He bought them all a round of drinks and left them to discuss it among themselves.

But he knew he had them.

April was walking across from the saloon when Bert Raitt walked out. She stopped short, took a good long look to be sure that she was right, and then put her hands on her hips.

Pike saw April give the signal and looked where she was looking. He saw the man coming out of the saloon, and recognized him from her description.

Pike felt a coldness in the pit of his stomach as he stared at the man who had led the assault on Sun Rising.

Raitt turned to walk toward his house, then stopped and looked across the street. There was a blonde woman there, looking his way. Abruptly, she turned and continued to walk, but he thought he had recognized her—but from where?

From where?

April saw Raitt turn her way and started walking. Under normal circumstances she might have approached him, might have attempted to do business, but Pike had warned her not to make contact with him.

What had this man done to Pike, to make the big mountain man want to kill him so badly?

She wondered if she would ever be able to get Pike to tell her that.

Pike stood his ground as Bert Raitt came toward him. There was no reason to hide from the man, because they had never met. If Raitt lived here at Pierre's Hole, he would still recognize Pike as a stranger, but as far as Raitt knew he had nothing to fear from a stranger.

The man glanced at Pike as he passed, and Pike studied his eyes. Raitt didn't look back as he passed, didn't see Pike staring at his retreating back. Pike's hand itched to take his Kentucky pistol from his belt and shoot Raitt in the back. It was the kind of fate the man deserved.

He watched as Raitt got farther and farther away, and then turned a corner and vanished from sight.

He turned to find April coming toward him.

Raitt turned the corner and fought a strong urge to look back. He knew he had seen the woman before, but he couldn't remember where. It would come to him, though. Sooner or later. It always did.

He had seen the big man, too, but had only glanced

at him in passing. Long enough to know that the man was a stranger, but not long enough to notice that the man seemed interested in him.

"That was him," she said.

"I know."

"He saw me."

"Did he recognize you?"

"I don't know."

"He saw me, too," Pike said, "but he paid no attention to me."

"That's good, isn't it?" she asked.

"Yes," Pike said, "that's very good."

He took her arm.

"Come on, let's go find McConnell and Buck."

They found the camp north of Pierre's Hole, in a clearing behind some trees.

McConnell had a fire going, and there was a pot of coffee on it.

"Did you find him?" he asked as Pike and April entered camp.

"We found him," Pike said. "He saw April."

"Did he recognize her?"

"I don't know," Pike said.

"Well, even if he does," McConnell said, "why would he care. Excuse me, April, but he's just got to figure that there's a new whore in the Hole."

"Is that what you're going to do here?" Pike asked. "Work as a whore?"

"It's what I do," she said to Pike. "It's honest work, isn't it?"

"It is that," Pike said. "Honest and hard."

"So why shouldn't I?"

"No reason," he said. "Didn't you say that Raitt had a wife here?"

"That's what I heard."

"So then even if he recognized you as a whore, he won't be approaching you for your services."

April allowed herself a wry smile and said, "You'd be surprised how many of my customers are married men, Pike. Sometimes they just can't get what they want at home."

"I wonder if Raitt is that kind of man?" McConnell asked.

"Well, if he approaches me," she said, "I'll let you know."

"You do that," McConnell said.

"I'm going back to my hotel."

"If you go for something to eat," Pike said, "remember what I told you. It's better for you if no one knows you came to town with us."

"I'll remember."

As she walked away from camp McConnell said, "Should we let her go?"

"Why not?" Pike asked. "She shouldn't be in any danger. As far as Raitt's concerned, she's just a whore."

"Did he see you?"

"He did," Pike said, pouring himself a cup of coffee. "He walked right by me — close enough for me to touch."

"Or kill."

"That's right," Pike said, "or kill."

April wanted to go back to her hotel, but her stomach wouldn't let her. She decided to have something to eat after all.

Over dinner she thought about what her life would be like in Pierre's Hole. She didn't know how long she would stay here, but she wanted to live well while she did. The only commodity she had to sell was her body—and maybe while she was doing business, she could do something to help Pike.

Why she should help him at all she didn't know. Sure, he had taken her along with him to Pierre's Hole, but she had paid him for that in advance, with the information about Raitt.

So why should she help him now?

She didn't know for sure. All she did know was that she wanted to.

And maybe he'd be able to help her get what she wanted, as well.

When Raitt returned to his cabin Rae was awake.

"There you are," she said. "I was wondering—"

"I went for a walk," he said, kissing her forehead.

"What do you want for dinner?"

"We're going out for dinner," he said, putting his arms around her from behind.

"We are? Where?"

"The Kents invited us."

"Oh," Rae said, "I've got to find something to wear."

He released her so that she could go and check her limited wardrobe.

"I like the Kents, Bert," she said, her back to him, "don't you?"

"Oh yes," he answered without hesitation, thinking of Leanne. "I like them a lot."

CHAPTER TWENTY-THREE

Dinner was a strained affair, at best, and Leanne couldn't believe that she was the only one who felt it.

She found herself seated directly across from Bert Raitt, and it seemed that every time she looked his way, he was staring at her.

Leanne tried to avoid speaking to Raitt so she wouldn't have to look at him, and kept talking with Rae about her baby.

"Don't you want to have children, Leanne?" Rae asked at one point.

"Oh, of course I do," Leanne said.

"They say women are more beautiful when they're pregnant," Bert said to Leanne. "Don't you think so, Leanne?"

Leanne looked at Raitt, unable to avoid it since he had spoken directly to her.

"You only have to look at your wife, Bert," she said more sharply than she intended, "to know that's true."

"Yes," Raitt agreed, causing his wife to smile, "I can see that very clearly."

"Well," Jesse Kent said, "I don't see how Leanne could get any more beautiful."

"I agree with you, Jesse," Rae said. "Don't you agree, Bert?"

Bert Raitt looked directly at Leanne Kent and said, "Oh, I agree, totally."

Leanne shivered, and wondered why nobody else did.

"What's wrong, honey?" Jesse asked.

"I'm just cold."

"I'm a little cold, too," Rae said.

"I'll stoke up the fire," Jesse said, sliding his chair back and standing up.

"I'll get the coffee," Leanne said. She didn't want to be sitting at the table alone with the Raitts.

"Leanne is acting awfully strange," Rae said to Raitt in a low voice.

"I think she's jealous of you," Raitt said.

"Of my fat belly?"

"Of your beauty," Raitt said, covering her hand with his.

Rae blushed at her husband's compliment. She pulled her hand away from his as both of the Kents returned to the table.

Pike accepted a plate of beans from McConnell and handed it to Buck. He accepted another and started eating.

"Now that we know he's here," McConnell said, "what do we do now?"

"We wait."

"Wait?"

Pike nodded.

"Why wait with this one?" McConnell asked. "You killed the others quick enough."

"This one was the leader," Pike said. "The others did what he told them to do."

"So? All the more reason to kill him quickly."

"No," Pike said, "slowly, after I find out what he's doing here, what he's got."

"Oh, I see," McConnell said. "You don't just want to kill him, you want to do to him what he did to you."

"What's wrong with that?"

"What are you going to do?" McConnell asked. "Kill his wife?"

Pike glared at McConnell.

"That's what it sounds like, Pike," McConnell said, in self defense.

"I just want to watch him, see what he's got here in Pierre's Hole."

"You mean, besides his wife?"

"Yeah, besides his wife," Pike said. "I want to see if he's got a life here."

"And then you'll take it away from him."

"That's what I came all this way for, isn't it, Skins?" Pike asked. "To take his life?"

"Yeah, that's what you came for."

"You know," Pike said, "you and Buck can leave now. I can do this alone."

"What about Tilson?"

"He'll come," Pike said. "Raitt does his thinking for him. Sooner or later, he'll come back."

"Yeah, well, I'll stick around for a while," McConnell said, "if you don't mind. I'd like to see how it all comes out."

"Suit yourself," Pike said.

"Yeah," McConnell said, "I always do . . . don't I?"

Pike looked at McConnell, then smiled and said, "Yeah, Skins, yeah, you do."

Buck had been staring at both men. They'd been talking too fast for him to follow all of it, but he had been listening to their tone of voice. When the voices became friendly again, he went back to his beans.

191

Later that night, Pike was looking at the sky while behind him McConnell and Buck were sleeping on the ground, wrapped in their blankets.

Pike was staring at the stars, trying to bring Sun Rising's face back. The only thing he could see, though, was her face the last time he saw her, burned and still, lifeless. He couldn't seem to bring her face back into focus, smiling and alive.

He guessed that he'd always remember her the way she was that last time. For that, he owed Bert Raitt. He had taken away Sun Rising's life, and Pike was going to do the same thing to him.

A life for a life.

Tilson knew he was close to Pierre's Hole. If he rode a few hours more he'd be there, but it was dark now, and he didn't want to ride in the dark. Morning would come soon enough. He could ride in, find Raitt and then together they could decide what to do.

PART FIVE

A LIFE FOR A LIFE

CHAPTER TWENTY-FOUR

In the morning Pike was wondering how he could find out where Bert Raitt lived without actually asking anyone. He didn't want anyone remembering later on that he'd been asking for him.

He posed the question to McConnell, who thought about it a few minutes.

"Well, I could follow him."

"Why you?" Pike asked.

"Well, you can't do it, you're too big," McConnell said. "He'd spot you in the minute. Buck's small enough to do it without being noticed, but he's an Indian."

"So that leaves you."

"Right. I'll just wander around some until I see him, and then stay with him."

"Okay," Pike said, "and what do I do in the meantime?"

"Hey, that's up to you," McConnell said. "Stay around here and get some rest."

"Some rest?"

"Yeah," McConnell said, "rest, relax. You been driving yourself pretty hard for the past month or so.

Maybe you should take a day to just . . . do nothing."

Pike thought about that, and raised his eyebrows. If McConnell was going to follow Raitt, there really wasn't all that much for Pike to do. Taking it easy might be a good idea.

"Talk to Buck," McConnell said, "get to know him a little bit. You'll find he's a pretty smart kid."

"He is, huh? Have you decided what you're going to do with him, yet?"

"No, I haven't," McConnell said. "Maybe I'll just keep him around."

"For what?"

McConnell shrugged and said, "I'll let you know when I figure it out. I'm going to get going."

"Be careful, Skins," Pike said. "We already know what this man is like."

"I'll be careful," McConnell said. "I'm always careful."

Pike watched as McConnell walked away, then turned around and looked at Buck, who was still eating his breakfast.

"Buck," Pike said, and the boy looked up, "we need some meat. How would you like to go hunting?"

The boy's eyes lit up and he nodded his head vigorously.

McConnell wandered around Pierre's Hole as the place came alive. People went about their business, barely giving him a second glance. He passed one or two of the people who had been in the restaurant yesterday, but they didn't pay him much mind, either.

About ten a.m. he finally spotted Bert Raitt.

Raitt woke in a bad mood.

196

He slid from bed without waking Rae and went outside. He'd slept late, and that always put him in a bad frame of mind, but it was more than that. He'd dreamt about Leanne Kent . . .

. . . In the dream he went to the Kent house and found Leanne there all alone. He knocked on the door and when she answered it he pushed her inside.

"Jesse will be back soon," she said, fear in her voice.

"If he comes back," Raitt had said, "I'll kill him. He won't bother us."

"What do you mean — " she started to ask, but he cut her off by pushing her down on the bed. He took hold of her shirt and tore it open. In his dream her breasts looked the way he thought they'd look, little peach tits with pink nipples.

She started to breathe harder and he knew then that she wanted him, that she had always wanted him.

He opened her pants, pulled them off her long, lean legs, and then tore her underwear off. He had his own pants down and his penis was harder and bigger than it had ever been before. As he mounted her, she opened her mouth even as he spread her legs apart, probably to ask him for it . . . and then he woke up . . .

. . . He was still hard when he woke up.

It was more than the dream, though. It was that damn restless feeling. It was gnawing at his insides, trying damn hard to get out, and he didn't know how much longer he could keep it in.

He decided to go for a long walk — as soon as his damn erection went down!

Pike and Buck went hunting on foot. Hunting had always relaxed Pike in the past, and it was almost working this time. He missed two shots, one at a rabbit and the other at a deer. He wasn't concentrating.

"This time," Pike told Buck, "I won't miss."

Buck nodded.

"I don't usually miss."

"I know," the boy said.

Pike looked at the boy in surprise.

"How do you know that?"

"Skins told me."

"That I don't usually miss?"

"That you never miss," Buck said.

"Never?"

Buck nodded.

"I guess you're not real impressed, then."

"Skins says that you are going through a lot," Buck said. "He says you are a fine man who has taken the wrong path. Is that true?"

Pike frowned. "If Skins said so, then it must be true. He's a very wise man."

"He says the same about you."

"He does?"

"Yes," Buck said, "most of the time."

With his next shot Pike took down a deer in full flight.

Rae Raitt was carrying firewood into the house when she saw the man and Indian boy emerging from the woods. At first she was intrigued to see a white man with an Indian boy. Then her attention was attracted to the deer the man was carrying over his shoulders.

The man and the boy stopped short when they saw her.

"Can I help you?" she said.

Pike stopped short, shocked. The last thing he expected to see was a pregnant woman—a very pregnant woman—collecting firewood.

He couldn't think of anything to say until she asked him if she could help him.

"Uh, no," he said, "but maybe I can help you."

"Oh? How?" The woman seemed nervous, and he wanted to put her at ease.

"Well, you shouldn't be carrying firewood in your condition," Pike said, putting the deer down. "Can I— uh, we take it in for you?"

The woman studied him for a moment, then looked at the boy, who was staring at her belly.

"All right," she said. "I would appreciate it."

Once they had the wood inside she offered him a cup of coffee, and gave the boy some candy.

"Are you just passing through?" she asked.

"Yes," Pike said. "We camped outside of town. We'll be leaving in a few days."

"I see."

"When is the baby due?"

She touched her belly lovingly and said, "In a few weeks."

"I wish you good luck," he said, standing up. "Thanks for the coffee."

"You're welcome," she said. "Thank you for taking the wood in."

"It was nothing. Come on, Buck."

Buck, who hadn't spoken a word, followed him to the door.

"Is Buck your son?" she asked.

"No," he said, "he's just—no, he's not my son."

"Oh."

He opened the door, then turned to her and said,

"Listen, we've got a whole deer out there, and we'll never use all the meat. How about if I cut some for you?"

"Oh, you don't have to do that . . ."

"It's all right," Pike said. "I want to. Besides, you've got to eat right if you're going to have a healthy baby."

She smiled. "Thank you, Mr. . . . ?"

"Pike," he said, "my name is Jack Pike. I'll just cut it up outside and leave it for you."

"Thanks."

"That's all right," he said. "I hope you and your husband enjoy it, Mrs. . . . ?"

"Raitt," she said, "my name is Rae Raitt. My husband's name is Bert, and I'm sure he'll enjoy it."

"Yes," Pike said, his voice devoid of inflection, "yes, I'm sure he will."

McConnell hardly had to move to keep Raitt in sight. The man seemed to be wandering aimlessly, and barely exchanged a word with anyone. When the saloon opened at noon, he went inside and stayed there for a long time. McConnell stood outside. He decided against going in, because that would cause Raitt to take note of him. He decided to wait outside and hope that when the man left the saloon he'd head home.

After that, McConnell would go into the saloon himself and get a drink.

Raitt had a drink, and then he had another. He didn't think he'd ever drunk this early in all the years he'd lived in Pierre's Hole. He was going to have to think of an explanation for Rae, who would smell it on him when he got home. He'd just tell her that the closer he came to being a father, the more nervous he was getting.

He finished the drink he had in front of him and decided against having another. If he had to explain it to her drunk, he might not sound so convincing.

He left the saloon and headed home.

Pike and Buck were roasting deer meat when McConnell returned later that afternoon.

"Well," McConnell said, eyeing the venison, "it looks like you put the time to good use."

"We did."

McConnell sat down opposite Pike, who was staring at the meat.

"Aren't you going to ask me?"

"Ask you what?" Pike said.

"If I found out where Bert Raitt lives."

"East of the Hole proper," Pike said. "A small cabin, with a very pregnant wife waiting for him inside."

McConnell stared.

"How did you – how did you know his wife was pregnant? I only noticed that because she opened the door for him. I guess she was waiting for him to come back."

"Buck and I went hunting, walked a long way. We decided to try a shorter route, and came across a pregnant woman trying to carry firewood."

"His wife?"

"Rae Raitt," Pike said, "wife of Bert Raitt. Hell, we even left her some meat."

McConnell sat stunned for a moment, then smiled.

"What's so funny?" Pike asked.

"I'm sorry, Pike," McConnell said, "it's just that you supplied Bert Raitt with tonight's dinner. That's kind of ironic, isn't it?"

"I suppose it is."

McConnell frowned.

"So what's botherin' you?"

Pike didn't answer.

"Not so intent on killing Raitt now that you met his wife?"

Pike still didn't reply, and continued to stare at the cooking meat.

"Is it because she's pregnant?"

Pike's eyes came up quickly and he pinned McConnell with a hard stare.

"That's it, ain't it? You kill him and you leave her without a husband, and her baby without a father."

Pike took out his knife and stabbed viciously at the cooking meat.

"I guess you have a lot of thinking to do, my friend," McConnell said, softly, "a lot of thinking."

When Bert Raitt saw the fresh kill hanging outside the house he stopped short. Rae didn't know one end of a gun from the other, so she certainly couldn't have shot it — and if she had, she wouldn't have been able to carry or drag it home, not in her condition.

He approached the door, but it opened before he got there.

"Bert, I was worried — " Rae started, but Raitt cut her off.

"Where did the meat come from, Rae?"

"A man brought it."

"What man?"

"A man who was out hunting," she said. "He came as I was trying to bring some firewood in — "

"Why were you trying to bring firewood in?"

"Because we needed it, Bert," she said. "You forgot to bring it in last night."

"All right," he said, "all right, go on."

"Well, the man had been out hunting, and he offered to carry the wood in for me."

"And you let him?"

"Yes—"

"How many times have I warned you about strangers?"

"I know, but we needed the wood, and I couldn't carry it—"

"All right, never mind," he said. "What happened after that?"

"Well, I offered him coffee, and the boy candy—"

"Boy? What boy?"

"A young Indian boy the man had with him—"

"You invited an Indian into our home?"

"He was just a boy," she said. "I gave him some of my candy, and I gave the man some coffee. In return, he offered us some of the meat. I thought you'd be pleased, Bert. What's wrong?"

Raitt fought for control. If she had been one of his men who had disobeyed him, he would have known what to do, but she wasn't one of his men, she was his wife.

"Nothing," he said, "nothing's wrong. I just don't . . . like strangers."

"Bert, I'm sorry," she said. "Don't be angry. We needed the wood, and I tried but I couldn't carry it."

"I know, I know," he said, touching her hair. "I'm sorry, I should have brought it in last night."

"And we have meat for dinner. I was going to make you a nice dinner—" Tears started rolling down her cheeks and he took her in his arms.

"I know," he said, "it's going to be a great dinner . . ."

He soothed her, but in the back of his mind he was thinking about the man, and the boy . . .

Dan Tilson rode into Pierre's Hole and, never having been there before, he was impressed. The place was bigger than he thought it would be, and it wasn't going to be so easy to find Raitt without asking. He wasn't sure he wanted to ask, doing that might make Raitt even madder.

He left his horse at the small, makeshift livery and decided to have a drink before trying to find Raitt. He'd find Bert before he found a place to stay. Maybe Bert would even offer to put him up.

Dan Tilson had convinced himself that Raitt would be mad, but that he wouldn't be that mad. They hadn't seen each other in weeks, and wouldn't that mean something to Raitt? After all, they were friends.

CHAPTER TWENTY-FIVE

Pike went for a walk—alone.

He had expected to find Bert Raitt married. April Dancer had told him as much. What he hadn't expected was to find his wife pregnant.

Damn Raitt, anyway. How could such a man have a wife—and a wife with child, at that? And what did that do to Pike's plan for vengeance?

The answer was simple.

It didn't do anything. He couldn't allow it to stop him. He could feel sorry for the wife and the unborn child after he killed Raitt. For all Pike knew Sun Rising could have been pregnant when Raitt and his crew killed her.

Jesus . . . he hadn't thought of that before.

When Pike returned to camp, McConnell was sitting at the fire, drinking coffee.

"Where's Buck?" Pike asked.

"He's around," McConnell said. "He went for a walk. What did you two talk about while you were hunting?"

"You." Pike sat opposite his friend and poured a cup of coffee.

205

"Boring subject."

"Couldn't be as boring as what you and he were always talking about."

They exchanged amused glances then McConnell said, "What are you going to do about Raitt's wife?"

"I'm not going to do anything."

"That mean you're going to forget this?"

"It doesn't mean that at all," Pike said.

"You're going through with it?"

"Of course."

McConnell ran a hand over his jaw.

"What's the matter?" Pike asked.

"Nothing."

"Skins," Pike said, "Raitt's wife being pregnant doesn't make Sun Rising any less dead. You've got to agree with that."

"Sure," McConnell said, "I agree with that, but—"

"And something occurred to me a while ago that I hadn't thought of before."

"What's that?"

Pike told his friend how he'd been thinking that Sun Rising might have been pregnant.

"She wasn't, was she?" McConnell asked, looking stricken.

Pike hesitated a moment and said, "Not that I know of—but what if she was? You think those animals would have cared? You think they wouldn't have raped her? Would've let her live? Not a chance. Raitt's got to die, Skins."

"So, kill him and let's get it over with."

"No," Pike said, "not that fast."

"What do you have in mind?"

"He lives here," Pike said. "The people here—his neighbors—probably don't know anything about what he does when he's away."

"We're assuming he led that settlement massacre,

right?"

"Right," Pike said, "that and Sun Rising and who knows what else?"

"So you want to let his neighbors know what kind of man he really is?"

"Right."

"And his wife?"

"That's right."

"And then you'll kill him."

"Right again."

McConnell leaned forward and said, "And what's that going to do to his wife?"

Pike scowled. "I can't concern myself with that, Skins."

"The old Jack Pike would."

Pike stared at McConnell. "The old Jack Pike is gone."

Pike stood up, dumped the rest of his coffee onto the fire, and walked away.

"That's what I'm afraid of," McConnell said, to his friend's retreating back.

Raitt told Rae he was going down to the trading post to get some coffee. He was actually going into town to find out what he could about the tall white man with the Indian boy. Raitt didn't like the idea of a stranger coming into the Hole and just by coincidence running into his wife. When you made your living the way Bert Raitt did—lying, cheating, stealing, even killing—you were wary of strangers—and even more wary of strangers in your own home.

A man as big as Rae said this one was wouldn't be able to hide in the Hole.

Tilson stood at the bar with his second beer, still trying to work up the nerve to go and find Raitt. He was actually leaning toward riding out of the Hole before Raitt found him. He was starting to think that coming here wasn't such a good idea.

He finished his beer and turned to leave, but as he did the door opened and a man stepped in.

It was Bert Raitt.

Raitt stopped short as he entered the saloon. He couldn't believe his eyes.

Dan Tilson.

The bartender behind Tilson called out, "Hi, Bert. A beer?"

Raitt tore his eyes from Tilson and looked at the man behind the bar.

"Yeah, Roy, sounds good."

Raitt walked to the bar, passing Tilson as if he wasn't there. He hoped that Tilson would be smart enough not to approach him, not to let on that they knew each other.

Roy, the bartender, gave Raitt his beer.

"Roy, you seen any strangers around lately?"

"Well," Roy said, "there's this fella, of course."

Tilson turned and looked at Raitt, and Raitt regarded him as if he had never seen him before.

"You just passing through, fella?" Raitt asked.

Tilson swallowed and said, "That's right."

"Not much work around here, unless you live here," Raitt said. "You wanted to stay, you'd probably have to check with Del Beman, over at the trading post."

"The trading post," Tilson repeated.

"That's right."

"Well," Tilson said, "like I said, I'm just passin' through."

208

"Good luck to you, then," Raitt said.

"Thanks," Tilson said, and made his way haltingly to the door. Two or three times Raitt thought he was going to turn back around, but Tilson finally made it out the door.

"Aside from that fella, Roy," Raitt said, "see any strangers?"

"Well . . . not that I seen them, but I heard of a ruckus over at the restaurant yesterday."

"What kind of ruckus."

"Well, two strangers came into town, two white men, with an Indian boy. You know ol' Rafe, he don't like servin' Indians, but these fellas made him."

"What was the ruckus?"

"No ruckus, really," Roy said "Hal Garland and two of his friends said they didn't like eatin' with no Indians, and these two fellas stared Garland and the others down and tossed them out."

"Threw them out?"

"Well, not actually," the bartender corrected himself. "Garland and them walked out, but they woulda got tossed out, the way I heard it."

"Two men, huh?"

"That's what I heard."

Raitt tossed a coin onto the bar for the beer and said, "Thanks, Roy."

"Sure, Bert," Roy said, pocketing the coin, "anytime."

April Dancer was across the way from the saloon when the door opened and a man stepped out. April stopped short when she recognized him, and backed into a doorway so the man wouldn't see her. The man seemed unsure about which way to go, then turned to his left and started walking. April decided against fol-

209

lowing him. She decided it was more important to tell Pike that Dan Tilson was in town.

She was about to start walking when the saloon door opened again and Bert Raitt stepped into the street. He looked both ways, then turned to his right and walked as far as the restaurant, then went inside. April left the doorway and headed in the opposite direction.

Raitt went and spoke to the owner of the restaurant, Rafe Lewis. Rafe told him the same story Roy had told him, and then said, "Them two was mountain men, Raitt, and they was mean-lookin'."

"Thanks very much, Rafe."

"You know them fellers, Bert?"

"No," Bert Raitt said, "but I have a feeling I'm going to."

CHAPTER TWENTY-SIX

For a reason she didn't quite understand April was happy when she ran into Pike, walking alone.

"April," he said, surprised at seeing her. "Were you coming to camp?"

"Yes, I was."

"We can go back—"

"No," she said, "I have a feeling that what I have to say will be of more interest to you."

"All right," he said, "walk with me."

She fell into step beside him and they continued back the way she had come.

"So, what do you have to tell me?"

"I just saw Dan Tilson."

"What?" he said grabbing her elbow.

"Ow!"

He released her just as quickly as he had grabbed her.

"I'm sorry," he said. "Where did you see Tilson?"

"He was coming out of the saloon."

Pike looked away from her and said, "He must have gotten here today."

"Does that change your plans?"

"Some," Pike said, "it might change them some." He looked at her and asked, "Was anyone with him?"

"Not with him, but shortly after he came out of the saloon, Bert Raitt came out."

"You didn't see them together?"

"No, in fact, when they left the saloon they went separate ways."

"Raitt probably doesn't want to be seen with Tilson," Pike said, "but they'll have to meet somewhere. Raitt will want to know why Tilson is here."

"Do you know why Tilson is here?"

Pike stared at April for several seconds. Tilson might have found out about the deaths of Haywood, Hecox and Murphy, and he was panicking.

"I might," Pike said.

April waited to see if Pike would continue. When he didn't, she said, "Okay, none of my business."

She turned to walk away. "Wait, April, wait," Pike said.

She stopped, but didn't turn around. The set of her shoulders told him that she was either angry or hurt — or both.

"Look . . . there are things I could tell you that you wouldn't want to hear . . ."

"Like what?" she asked, turning. "I already know that you plan to kill Tilson and Bert Raitt. You've killed the others already."

Pike hesitated a moment, then said, "Three, three others. Men who rode with Tilson and Raitt."

"Rode with them? And did what?"

"They raped and killed my woman, and burned down our home."

She stared at him.

"Your wife?"

"We weren't married," he said. "She was a Crow woman, and she lived with me."

212

"And they . . . did this to her?"

"Yes."

"How do you know it was them?"

"Because Buck saw them," Pike said.

"I see," she said, "and that's why he travels with you. To identify them?"

"Yes."

"Oh, Pike—"

"That's not all," Pike said. "Have you heard about what they're calling the 'settlement massacre?' "

"Yes, I have. I—you mean, they did that, too?"

"I don't have any proof," Pike said, "but I think they did that, and a lot more. When they're finished with their raping and killing, they separate and hide out."

"And this is where Raitt goes to hide?"

"Yes," Pike said. "I think Bert Raitt has an entirely different life here, and I don't think anyone knows what he does when he's away. He keeps that part of his life secret."

"Well, if that's the case," April said, "then Raitt is not going to be very happy to see Tilson here."

"No," Pike said, "I don't guess that he will . . ."

As Raitt approached the trading post he saw Tilson loitering about out front.

He walked past Tilson and said, "Meet me out back."

Raitt went inside and bought a pound of coffee. Then he went out the front door, looked around, made sure that no one was watching him, and walked around behind the trading post, where he found Dan Tilson waiting nervously.

"Bert—" Tilson said, but Raitt cut him off with a right hand that struck him flush in the face.

Raitt stood over the fallen Tilson with his legs spread

wide.

"What the hell are you doing here?" he demanded.

"Now wait, Bert," Tilson said, holding his hands out in front of him, "I came so we could figure out what to do —"

"Do? About what?" Raitt asked. "Do you know what you're doing by coming here? You're endangering my life here."

"Look," Tilson said, "look, the word has gotten out about —" he lowered his voice here — "about what we done."

"Shut up!" Raitt said. He reached down, grabbed Tilson by the shirt and hauled him to his feet.

"Don't hit me again, Bert!" Tilson pleaded.

Raitt considered hitting him again, then pushed him back against the wooden wall of the trading post.

"All right," Raitt said, "all right, you're here. I might be able to use you."

"For what?"

"I don't know, yet," Raitt said. "There was a stranger at my house today."

"What did he want?"

"I don't know."

Do you think he's from . . . from the settlement —"

"Shut up about that!" Raitt said. "There was nobody left there, we made sure of that. He can't be . . . Look, I want you to camp outside of the Hole and wait until you hear from me."

"What am I supposed to do?"

"I Just told you what to do," Raitt said, patiently. "Camp and wait. Don't come anywhere near here unless I send for you. Do you understand?"

"Yeah, yeah, I understand, Bert. Are we gonna do something —"

"We're going to do something, Dan," Raitt said. "I don't know what, yet. But when I do, I'll let you know."

"Okay, Bert," Tilson said, "whatever you say."

"Now get the hell out of here, and don't come around again."

Tilson nodded and started walking away. Abruptly, he turned and said, "It's really good to see you again, Bert."

"Get out of here!"

Pike and April found a couple of large stones to sit on. Pike told April about Raitt's wife.

"This has to be very difficult for you, Pike," April said. "I can't tell you what to do."

"I know that," Pike said. "I know what I have to do and I'll do it. I may not like it, I may not like myself after it's all over, but I'll do it."

"I'll still like you."

Pike looked at her.

"I didn't know you liked me at all."

"I didn't know how much I liked you . . . until now," she said.

"Even after I've told you that I killed three men, and I intend to kill two more? Even though by killing one of them I'm leaving a woman and a baby alone in the world?"

April stared at the ground for a few moments, and then looked up at him.

"That will be her pain," she said, "and she'll have to live with it, the way you've been living with your pain."

"But I haven't been living with my pain," Pike said, "I've been killing with it."

"That's your way of dealing with it," April said. "I know that kind of pain, Pike."

"Do you?"

"I've lost someone I loved in the past, so yes, I do

know. You do whatever you have to do to make that kind of pain bearable."

"No matter what the expense?"

She leaned over and touched his arm.

"You already know the answer to that."

Raitt was sure now that the strangers weren't staying inside the Hole. That meant that they had made camp somewhere outside.

He figured he could work this one of two ways. He could wait and see if they made some kind of contact again, with him or with Rae. Or, he could go and make contact with them himself and find out just what they wanted — if they wanted anything. They could have just been strangers passing through, who accidentally stumbled onto Rae and wanted to help her, because of her condition. If that was the case, then they meant him no harm, and he'd mean them no harm.

It wasn't possible that they could be witnesses, or survivors, of the settlement he and his men had wiped out. They had remained in that settlement for a week, making sure they knew every face. Raitt and his men knew that they had killed every man, woman and child inside that settlement.

Could they be looking for him for some other offense? The only way to find that out was to go to them and ask them. For that he'd need not only Tilson behind him, but his three new protegès, as well.

He left the rear of the trading post and went to find Kincaid, Newman and Peters.

CHAPTER TWENTY-SEVEN

The last place Pike expected to find himself was in the small room that April had rented at the Hole's poor excuse for a hotel.

Actually, compared to the accommodations offered by other mountain settlements, Pierre's Hole was the St. Louis of the mountains.

April had taken his hand and walked him back to the hotel and up to her room, without a word.

Inside the room he could see that she had a small pallet to sleep on, one that would never hold both of them. He also saw that the floors were hardpacked dirt, and not wood.

She took the blanket off the pallet and spread it on the floor, looking at him with a smile. She then proceeded to undress.

Dressed she looked slim, but as she removed her clothing, her breasts suddenly sprang free, larger and fuller than he expected. They were pale, with small, pink nipples. She leaned down to remove her pants, and her breasts swung a bit, slapping together. She let her pants drop to the ground, revealing a flat belly and deep navel. When she removed her underwear, he could see that the hair between her legs was as golden as the hair on her head.

"Now you," she said, moving closer to him. "I'll help you."

She undid his clothes and helped him remove them, until he was as naked as she was. She ran her hands over his shoulders, his rock hard biceps, his slab of a chest, then slid them down and took hold of his rigid cock.

"It's like a tree trunk," she said, squeezing it. "You're the biggest man I've ever seen."

She was a whore, and he didn't know whether she was telling the truth or not—but he didn't care.

He reached for her, grabbed her buttocks, and lowered her to the blanket. He kissed her nipples, licking them at first, then biting and sucking them. He ran his lips and tongue between her glorious breasts, kissed her shoulders, her neck, and then her mouth, which returned his kiss hungrily.

He was aware the whole time that she was a whore, and that she did this for a living, but it didn't matter to him. He needed to get away from everything for awhile, and he decided to stop thinking and just enjoy.

He mounted her, and she reached down, took him in one hand and rubbed the swollen tip of him against her vagina, wetting it. He thrust his hips forward and slipped halfway inside of her. She closed her eyes and caught her breath as he continued to move into her, slowly, inch by inch, until finally he was nestled full-hilt, his wiry black pubic hair mixing with her feathery golden hair.

He took his weight on his hands, which were flat on the ground to either side of her, and began to move slowly inside of her. She moaned softly and reached behind him, cupping his buttocks.

"Oh God," she said, "your ass is so hard, like stone."

He didn't say anything—he didn't know what to say to that. He just kept moving in her, and she arched her back and licked her lips as he began to move faster and faster.

"Ooh, um . . ." she said, as if she were eating something delicious. "Oh yes, Pike, um, ooh yes . . ."

She began to move her hips in unison with his, lifting hers to meet his thrusts. She released his buttocks and pressed her hands flat on the ground so she could lift her hips even higher.

"Your weight," she said then, "I want to feel your weight . . ."

"I'm heavy . . ." he said.

"Come on, come on . . ." she urged. "I won't break . . ."

He lowered his body until he was resting right on her, then slid his hands under her to cup her buttocks. Holding her that way, he began to penetrate her even more deeply, and she gasped, her mouth open, her tongue running over her lips.

"Oh, Jesus . . ." she said, beginning to buck beneath him, "Oh God, yes, oh yes, here it comes, I feel it, oh God, yes, yes . . ."

She kept up a steady stream of words, most of them right into his ear, some of them obscene . . . and then she bucked beneath him until he exploded inside of her, at which time she wrapped her arms and legs around him tightly, squeezed her eyes shut and bit him on the shoulder . . .

"I didn't break the skin," she said, moments later. She was running her finger over the spot on his

219

shoulder where she had bitten him.

"It's all right," he said.

She kissed the spot and propped herself up on her elbow, looking down at him.

"I think you needed that," she said.

"You're probably right."

"You might not believe this," she said, resting her hand on his chest, "but I needed that, too."

"I believe you."

She smiled. "I don't know if you really do or not, but it's true. What I needed was a mindless roll in the hay with someone I liked. You know, after doing this for a living, sometimes you think you've forgotten how to feel." She leaned down and kissed him gently on the mouth.

"What was that for?"

"That was for showing me that I haven't forgotten how to feel," she said. "Thank you."

"You're welcome," he said.

He sat up then and looked around for his clothes.

"Do you have to go?" she asked.

"Yes," he said, without looking at her, "I have to go."

He stood up and began to dress. She remained on the floor, watching him.

When he was dressed he tucked his Kentucky pistol into his belt.

"What will you do now?" she asked.

"I haven't decided, yet," he said. "I'll probably look for Tilson, to see where he's staying."

"Where do you think he'll stay?"

"Raitt will probably tell him to camp somewhere outside the settlement" Pike said. "He won't want him right in the Hole. He won't want anyone to see them together."

"Will you kill Tilson first."

He didn't really want to discuss this with her.

"April . . ."

"I know," she said, interrupting him, "it's none of my business."

"I don't want to get you any more involved."

"I understand," she said. "It's for my own protection, right?"

"That's right."

"All right, then," she said, "go and do what you have to do."

"What will you do now?" he asked.

"You mean will I go back to my old trade?" she asked. "Did you think one time with you would cure me of all that?"

"No, that's not what I meant."

"Well, the truth is," she said, "I haven't decided what I'm going to do. I guess we both have a lot of thinking to do."

"I guess we do."

"And I guess we'd better get to it."

He nodded, and turned toward the door.

"I'll let you know what I decide," she said, quickly, "if you'll let me know what you decide."

He looked over his shoulder at her. "Deal," he said and left.

McConnell had warned Buck not to go near any of the people in Pierre's Hole, but Buck was as curious as any young boy. He was curious about these white people. He was curious about the wooden teepees they lived in—and he was hoping to catch another whiff of steak cooking. The steak he'd had the first day they arrived was the most delicious thing he had ever tasted.

He was walking toward the restaurant when he saw

Bert Raitt. He hurriedly sought cover behind a wall and watched as Raitt walked to the saloon. He thought back to the last time he'd seen Raitt. He had been standing outside Pike's cabin, while his men were inside with Sun Rising. Buck could still hear her screaming as they raped her—although at the time, he really didn't know what they were doing to her. That was why he had moved closer to the cabin and peered inside the window. He had seen Sun Rising, lying on the floor naked. One man was holding her hands pinned to the floor, while two others held her legs. The fourth man, his pants down around his ankles, had been on top of her, his hips pumping up and down . . . In fear, Buck had run and hidden, not understanding what was going on, except that the men were hurting Sun Rising.

Later, after they had set fire to the cabin and rode off he had gone to see if he could help her, but the flames were too hot, and he couldn't get inside the cabin.

He felt ashamed then, and felt ashamed now—and he felt that the cause of his shame was this man Pike and McConnell called Raitt.

He wished he could kill Raitt himself, but he settled for following him.

CHAPTER TWENTY-EIGHT

Bert Raitt found Kincaid and Newman in the saloon, seated at a table, a beer in front of each of them. Peters wasn't with them.

"Where's Peters?" Raitt asked.

"He'll be along shortly," Kincaid said. "What's on your mind?"

Raitt sat down with them.

"Remember what we talked about the other day?"

"What?" Newman asked.

"Making money, stupid," Kincaid said. He looked at Raitt and said, "I remember. What about it?"

"Before I let you guys work with me in a big job, I've got to make sure you can do what you're told."

"How do we do that?" Kincaid asked.

"Well, there's a couple of strangers in town," Raitt said. "They came in with an Indian boy. Have you seen them around?"

"Not me," Kincaid said. "You?"

"Not me," Newman said.

"Well, you won't be able to miss them. One of them is big."

"Oh yeah?" Kincaid said. He was a big man himself, six foot two and over two hundred and twenty pounds. "I like big men—I like pounding on them."

"Well, pound on this one," Raitt said. "I want him and his friend to leave Pierre's Hole."

"Why?" Kincaid asked.

Raitt looked directly at the man.

"If you're going to work for me, you've got to lose that word."

"What word?"

"Why?" Raitt said. "The word 'why.' I don't like hearing it."

"Well, why—uh, what do we get out of this?" Kincaid asked.

"For starters, I'll pay you twenty dollars each. You, Newman and Peters."

"Twenty dollars?" Newman asked, his eyes widening.

"Take it easy," Kincaid said to his friend. He leaned forward and said, "I don't call twenty dollars a lot of money, Raitt."

"I said the twenty was for starters," Raitt said. "I just want to see how you do."

At that point Peters came walking into the saloon, a puzzled frown on his face.

"What's the matter with you?" Kincaid asked.

"On my way over here I saw a kid," he said, sitting down.

"So?"

"It was an Indian kid."

"A Crow Indian?" Raitt asked.

"I don't know," Peters said. "An Indian."

"What was he doing?"

"Well, he was standing out front, and I could swear he was listening to something."

"Where is he now?"

224

"He took off just as I was gettin' here."

"Did he see you?"

"No, he just took off."

"Which way?"

"North."

"One of you get out of here and find that kid," Raitt said. "He'll lead you to the others."

"What's goin' on?" Peters asked.

"Johnny," Kincaid said to Newman, "find that kid. I'll fill Bo in."

"All right," Newman said, "but don't lose my twenty dollars."

As Newman made for the door Peters asked, "What twenty dollars?"

Raitt stood up and said, "Kincaid will explain it." He took sixty dollars out of his pocket and handed it to Kincaid.

"If you don't get the job done," he said, "I'm gonna want that back."

"If we don't do the job, you'll get it back," Kincaid said, taking the money, "but we'll do it."

"What job?" Peters asked.

"Kincaid will explain it," Raitt said. "I'll be back here later to see how you did."

Raitt left the saloon. He looked down the road and saw Newman, who was moving like he had spotted the kid. Raitt decided to follow them both.

Newman trailed Buck, who led him right to Pike and McConnell's camp. McConnell was present, but Pike wasn't. Newman watched as the kid rushed to McConnell and started talking.

Newman turned and ran back to the saloon.

Raitt secreted himself so that Newman wouldn't

see him when he ran by. After that he moved closer to the camp and watched Buck and McConnell.

Raitt hoped that Newman had gone back to the saloon for the other two.

In the meantime, Raitt decided to try and find the big man himself.

"Slow down, Buck," McConnell said, "I can't understand what you're sayin'."

"The man, the leader—"

"Raitt?"

"Yes, Rat," Buck said, mispronouncing the name. "He meet with two men in saloon."

"Two men?" McConnell asked. "Not one?"

"Two," Buck said. "Mean men."

"Mean-looking?"

"Yes, mean-looking."

"What were they talking about?"

Buck shrugged.

"I did not hear them, but Rat, he did most of the talking."

McConnell frowned. Raitt could have simply been having a conversation with two of his neighbors.

"Buck," McConnell said, "have you seen Pike?"

"No."

"All right, Buck," McConnell said, "why don't you take me to those men."

They started to their feet and found themselves facing three men.

"There," Buck said.

Uncomfortably, McConnell realized that his rifle was next to his blanket, which was a good twenty feet from where he was.

"What can I do for you fellas?"

"It's not what you can do for us," Kincaid said, "but what we can do for you."

"And what's that?"

"We can deliver a message."

"From who?"

"That we can't say."

"Then what's the message?"

"Get out of Pierre's Hole."

"All right," McConnell said, "you delivered it."

"Maybe you didn't understand—" Kincaid said, but McConnell cut him off.

"I understood," he said. "You had a message to deliver, and you've delivered it. Now you can move on."

Kincaid looked at the other two men, who looked amused. "See? He didn't understand." He looked back at McConnell and said, "You see, you're the one who has to move on. You and your friend and your little heathen."

McConnell eyed the three men and decided not to play it hard.

"All right," McConnell said. "When my friend comes back, we'll move on."

"Is that a fact?" Kincaid said.

"That's a fact."

Kincaid studied McConnell for a few moments, then looked at his friends.

"I don't believe him, fellas. You believe him?"

"I don't believe him," Newman said.

"Me, neither," Peters said.

"Let's try to make it a little clearer," Kincaid said, and the three men started toward McConnell.

"Buck," McConnell said. "get behind me . . ."

227

It was at that moment that Pike stepped out of the hotel. He looked around, unsure of himself for the first time in a long time.

If he was Raitt, where would he tell Tilson to go? That wasn't too hard. He'd tell him to camp far away from the settlement and stay away until he sent for him.

Where would Tilson go? North, south, east or west? North or south. To pick east or west would require some imagination. If Dan Tilson had any imagination, he wouldn't be involved with a man like Bert Raitt.

North was out of the question, because he and McConnell were camped north. They would have seen Tilson. That left south, so Pike turned right and began to walk south.

McConnell did the best he could, but he was one against three.

The three men charged him, and he surprised them by charging right at them instead of moving away. He threw his shoulder into Newman, knocking the man off balance, and then swung left. Kincaid was faster than McConnell expected, though, and the man stiffarmed him, knocking *him* to the ground.

McConnell got to his feet and moved back around to where Buck was standing. He was concerned with the boy's welfare, which gave him a little *too* much to worry about.

The three men circled him, and then two of them charged. That left one — Kincaid — free to grab Buck. When Kincaid picked up poor Buck and threw him against a tree, McConnell's anger got the better of him, and he let his guard down. The three men swarmed over him and drove him to the ground. They began kicking him and he felt the pain of each savage blow until one of them kicked him in the head, and he didn't feel anything at all.

PART SIX

RETRIBUTION

CHAPTER TWENTY-NINE

Pike had walked a hundred feet and decided that he'd do better on horseback. He walked to the small livery shack, saddled his horse, and started south again. He reached the same point when something else occurred to him. He turned around and rode to the trading post and made a purchase. That done he finally rode south, and kept going.

Raitt spotted Pike riding away. He knew it was him because of his size. There was nobody else in town that big, not even Kincaid.

The big stranger was riding south, and if he kept riding south he'd end up finding Dan Tilson.

Bert Raitt figured that might not be so bad.

Tilson was sitting at his fire, nursing a cup of coffee. He was already growing bored, and wondered if it had been such a good idea to come to Pierre's Hole. If he hadn't come, he'd still be free to move around. This sitting in one place, waiting, was something he didn't do well.

When he heard the horse, he thought it was Raitt, and hoped that the waiting was over. He got up and walked out to meet Raitt.

But when the rider came into view, he saw that it wasn't Rait at all, but a stranger, a man who sat his horse taller than anyone Tilson had ever seen before.

The man's size intimidated Tilson, whose rifle was back by the fire.

"W-what can I do for you?"

Pike didn't answer. He dismounted and walked up to Tilson, staring the man in the face.

"Tilson?"

"That's right."

"Raitt sent me."

Tilson closed his eyes and breathed a sigh of relief.

"Bert sent you?"

"That's right."

"Come on into camp then," Tilson said. "You want a cup of coffee?"

"Sure."

Tilson walked back into camp with Pike behind him, leading his horse. Pike grounded the animal's reins and accepted a cup of coffee from Tilson.

"Does Bert want me to come back into Pierre's Hole?" Tilson asked.

"Not yet," Pike said. "Not for a while."

"Then why did he send you?"

"Well, he just wanted to make sure you were comfortable," Pike lied. "After all, it's kind of lonely out here, isn't it?"

"It sure is."

"He thought you might want someone to talk to."

"Well, that's right nice of Bert," Tilson said. "What's your name, friend?"

"Pike."

"Well, Pike, what are you doin' in Pierre's Hole?"

"Same thing you are," Pike said. "I'm waiting for Bert to set up his next job."

Tilson frowned.

"Is Bert recruiting some new men?"

"I guess so."

"He must have something big planned, then."

"I guess he must," Pike said. "Something like that settlement, only maybe a bigger one, huh?"

Tilson gave Pike a wary look and said, "He told you about the settlement, did he?"

"Well," Pike said, "when you're recruiting new men, you pretty much have to tell them what they're in for."

"I guess so."

"I mean," Pike said, "a man should always know what he's in for . . . don't you think so?"

"Oh, sure," Tilson said, "I couldn't agree with you more."

Pike took out his Kentucky pistol, pointed it at Tilson and said, "Good."

Raitt was still in the saloon when Kincaid and the others returned.

"Well?" he asked.

Kincaid spread his hands and said, "It's done."

"All of them?"

"No," Kincaid said, "the big tall one you mentioned wasn't there. We took care of the other one and the kid."

"Are they gonna leave Pierre's Hole?"

Kincaid laughed, and the other joined in.

"As soon as they can walk."

At that moment something seemed to snap inside Bert Raitt. It's as if the first act of violence in Pierre's Hole was all it took.

235

"All right," he said, breathing heavily, "all right, this is gonna be our big money day."

"But . . . the big one is still out there," Kincaid said.

"When you see him," Raitt said, "kill him."

"Kill him?" Newman asked.

"Yeah, is that too much for you to handle?"

Newman bristled and said, "Just tell us where the big money is gonna come from."

"Where's it gonna come from?" Raitt asked. "Look around you, men. It's gonna come from Pierre's Hole."

"This place?" Kincaid said. "We're gonna rob this place?"

Behind them the bartender was listening to this with a look of disbelief on his face.

"That's right," Raitt said, "and we might as well start right here."

Raitt pulled his pistol, turned and fired, catching the bartender in the forehead.

"Get whatever money he's got behind there," Raitt told them.

The three men stared at him in shock. Kincaid was the first to recover. He slapped the other two men on the back and said, "Let's move. Like the man said, 'today's our big money day.' "

April Dancer was confused. Pike had thrown her off balance. She didn't know if she wanted to make her living here the same way she'd made it in so many other places. She didn't know if she even wanted to stay here.

She wondered if Pike would agree to take her with him when he left.

Rae Raitt was worried.

Bert was acting strangely lately, and she couldn't figure out why. She decided that the only thing she could do was come out and ask him.

She grabbed her shawl, wrapped it around her, rubbed her swollen belly, and left the cabin to look for her husband.

Leanne Kent had a premonition. She'd never had one before, and this one frightened her.

Something was going to happen, that's all she knew. She was glad she was home with her husband.

Laura Boyd sat in a chair and stared at her husband, who was taking a nap on their bed. She stared, and stared, and stared, her mind racing.

She was growing old . . . too old, too fast, and she was starting to think that maybe Bert Raitt was her way out. Maybe by giving Bert Raitt what he wanted, she'd be able to hold onto what she wanted.

Her youth.

"What is this?" Tilson asked.

"This," Pike said, "is your last minute on earth, Tilson."

"W-wha—"

"I'm going to kill you."

"B-b-b-but . . . why?"

"Remember a Crow woman up near the Green River?" Pike asked. "You and Raitt, Haywood, Hecox, Murphy, you raped her, killed her and burned her cabin."

"S-so? She was an Indian."

"She was *my* Crow woman," Pike said, pressing the barrel of the pistol to Tilson's forehead, "and that was

237

my cabin, Tilson."

"W-w-what—"

"You're a dead man, Tilson," Pike said, "just like Hecox, and Haywood, and Murphy."

Tilson frowned.

"You—you killed them?"

"And I'm going to kill you," Pike said.

"Raitt will get you."

"Raitt will get his," Pike said. "I'm saving him for last."

"You can't—" Tilson said, and sprang from his seated position. His sudden move pushed Pike's pistol aside, and Pike took Tilson's weight on his chest. He went over backward, taking Tilson with him . . .

"Check outside," Raitt said.

While Newman and Peters collected the money that was behind the bar, Kincaid checked the street.

"It was only one shot," Kincaid said. "Didn't attract too much attention."

"Okay," Raitt said, having reloaded his pistol, "no more shooting. You all have knives?"

"Sure," Kincaid said.

"Now listen, and listen good. You take the restaurant, the trading post, the livery, and anyplace else that takes in money," Raitt said, ticking them off on his fingers. "You take them one at a time, and you don't use your guns. Understand?"

"Sure," Kincaid said, "we understand."

"If you make noise, or attract any attention, we're gonna have a lot of guns coming at us."

"We'll be quiet."

"And don't leave anyone alive."

"What?" Kincaid said, not sure he'd heard right.

"You heard me," Raitt said. "Each place you rob,

you kill the merchant, and any customers that might be there."

"Is that what you call not attracting attention?" Kincaid asked.

"Hey," Raitt said, "if we do this right, and fast enough, we'll be out of here before anyone notices anything. Anyone who sees you dies. Once we're out of here they won't be able to prove who did what. Understand?"

"Sure, Bert," Kincaid said, "I understand."

Raitt looked at Newman and Peters, who were still behind the bar.

"Understand?"

"Yeah," Newman said, exchanging a glance with Peters, "we understand."

"Then let's do it."

As he started for the door Kincaid said, "Where are you gonna be?"

"I've got some other things to take care of."

Raitt left the saloon, thinking about Leanne Kent and Laura Boyd. Not once did he think about his wife.

Pike stared down at Tilson, lying on the ground, lifeless, his head twisted at an unnatural angle. After his weight had carried Pike down to the ground they'd rolled around some, and Pike had come up behind Tilson. A twist of the neck, a loud crack, and Tilson was dead. It was the same way he had killed Murphy, and he was angry because that wasn't the way he had intended to kill Tilson.

He walked to his horse and took off the rope that was hanging on his saddle. The rope had been the last-minute purchase he made before leaving the Hole.

He dragged Tilson over to a tree and left him lying there. He made a noose on one end of the rope, then tossed it up and over a branch. He then leaned over and slid the noose around Tilson's neck. That done, he pulled, his muscles bunching. He was surprised at how light the man was. Hoisting his dead weight up by the neck was not as hard as he thought it would be.

When Tilson's feet cleared the ground and he was swaying, Pike tied his end of the rope off at the tree trunk. He stepped back and viewed his handiwork. If Raitt came out here to see Tilson, he'd find the man hanging, looking for all the word like someone who had been lynched.

He mounted up, took one last look, and rode away. Four of them were dead now, and that left only Raitt.

He wondered what Raitt was doing at that very moment.

CHAPTER THIRTY

Bert Raitt knocked on the door of Jesse and Leanne Kent's home. When Jesse Kent opened the door and saw Raitt he smiled.

"Hello, Bert—" he said, holding his hand, but he got no further. Raitt closed his hand over the younger man's, pulled him to him, and buried his knife to the hilt in his belly.

Jesse Kent never made a sound. He sagged against Raitt and died in his arms. Raitt lugged the body into the cabin.

"Oh my God," Leanne cried, as Raitt closed the door, "what happened?"

Raitt grinned at her and rolled Jesse over so she could see the knife sticking out of his belly.

"Oh no!" she wailed, putting her hands over her mouth. "What have you done?"

Raitt didn't answer her. Instead a sickly grin spread over his face, and as he started to unbuckle his belt she knew what he was going to do.

McConnell came to and crawled to where Buck was lying. The boy had hit the tree hard, and he was bleeding from the scalp, and mouth.

"Buck!" McConnell said. He shook the boy, and a stabbing pain went through his side. He knew from experience that he had at least one cracked rib, maybe more.

"Those sonsofbitches!" he said between his teeth.

They'd be after Pike next. Somehow, he had to warn him, and he had to get help for Buck.

Instead of riding back into Pierre's Hole, Pike by-passed it and rode directly to the camp. As he came within sight of it he saw McConnell and Buck, both on the ground, and he kicked his horse to a gallop.

He dismounted before the horse had stopped and ran to McConnell, kneeling by his friend.

"Skins! What happened?"

"Three men . . ." McConnell said, haltingly. "Told us to leave the Hole . . ."

"Were they sent by Raitt?"

"Don't know . . . why would they be . . ."

"Don't forget, his wife saw me. He may not like having a stranger come to his house, considering the way he makes his living. He may not know I'm after him, but he'd still want to try and scare us away."

"He's recruited some new men, then . . ." McConnell said.

"I guess so."

"How's the boy?"

Pike knelt over Buck and checked him.

"He's still alive. He's got a nasty cut on the head, but I think he'll be all right."

"Get goin'," McConnell said. "Get to them before they get to you."

McConnell described all three men as well as he could.

"I've got to get help for you and Buck."

"Just go," McConnell said. "I doubt there's a doctor

here. I'll do what I can for Buck."

"What about you?"

"I've had busted ribs before," McConnell said. "They hurt like hell, but they won't kill me. Go on, get moving. They're probably looking for you, now."

"I'll find Raitt," Pike said. "If I kill him first, the others will probably run."

"Maybe," McConnell said as Pike got up and mounted his horse, "but don't count on it . . ."

Pike rode back into Pierre's Hole and decided to try the saloon first. That was how he found the dead bartender. There was some money scattered on the floor, as if someone had hurriedly stuffed their pockets.

"They're robbing the Hole," he said to himself. "Another settlement massacre."

Not if he could help it.

"Bert, don't —" Leanne said.

"Come on, sweetheart," Raitt said to her. "You've wanted this for a long time."

"Bert . . . no!" she said, as he grabbed her by the shoulders.

Just like in his dream, he pushed her down onto the bed. In his dream she was wearing a shirt and pants, but now she was wearing a dress that buttoned up the front. He grabbed hold of it and ripped it open, then tore it from her body. Her breasts bobbed free, small as peaches, just like he thought. He pawed them, feeling the nipples as she struggled to get away from him.

"Bert —" she said, and he knew she was about to scream, so he backhanded her. Her eyes rolled up and she started to lose consciousness.

He tore off her underwear and she felt his fingers invade her. Semi-conscious, she tried to fight him, but she

243

was too weak.

He finished unbuckling his pants, pulled them down around his ankles, and climbed on the bed. He mounted her and drove his rigid penis home. She tried to scream, but he pressed one hand over her mouth. As she lay beneath him, gagged and helpless, he proceeded to brutally take her . . .

Rae Raitt wondered if her husband wasn't over at the Kents, maybe helping Jesse fix something else around the house. She decided that she would go over there and look for him. If he wasn't there, she could at least talk to Leanne.

Pike came out of the saloon and looked around. It was quiet, and there were people walking about as if nothing had happened. The bartender had been killed with a single shot, and he supposed that one shot could have gone unnoticed. He doubted, however, that they would have gotten enough money from the saloon to satisfy them.

He turned left and walked toward the trading post.

McConnell took his belt from his pants, then buckled it up around his ribs, making it as tight as he could. That done, he leaned over Buck and, using water from his canteen, cleaned the boy's face. The cut on his scalp wasn't as bad as it looked, once the blood was cleaned away, and the boy was breathing regularly.

He put a blanket under the boy's head, then picked up his rifle and started in the direction of Pierre's Hole, trying to ignore the pain that lanced through his side with every breath.

As Pike entered the trading post he stopped short of tripping over the body of a woman. She must have been unfortunate enough to walk in while they were robbing the place. She had blood all over her chest from a stab wound. He moved quickly to the counter and looked behind it. Sure enough, the owner was there, also stabbed to death.

They were going from store by store, using knives instead of guns, so that no one would notice.

He stepped over the woman, went out the door, took his pistol from his belt and fired it into the air. Just to be sure, he raise his rifle and fired it, too.

People noticed, and came running.

Kincaid watched while Newman and Peters killed the restaurant owner. Newman held him while Peters slit his throat. As they let the man's body fall to the ground they all heard the first shot, and then the second.

"What the hell — " Peters said. "There wasn't supposed to be any shooting."

"Get the money," Kincaid said. "We're gonna have to get out of here."

Pike reloaded his rifle as he explained to the people crowded around him what was happening.

"You men with rifles better start looking around," he said. "You others, get rifles and help. If you don't stop them, they'll destroy Pierre's Hole."

"Who's behind this?" a man asked.

"There's four men," Pike said, "but their leader is Bert Raitt."

"Raitt!" the man said. "But he lives here."

Pike slid his loaded pistol into his belt and said, "Not anymore."

245

When Kincaid, Peters and Newman came out of the restaurant they saw a group of men approaching, all of them armed.

"There they are!" someone shouted, and then the shooting started.

Pike heard the shots, but he left the saving of Pierre's Hole to its citizens.

He wanted to find Bert Raitt.

As Rae Raitt approached the home of the Kents, she heard a woman from inside. For a moment she thought that perhaps she'd be disturbing the Kents, but then the woman screamed, and it did not sound like a scream of pleasure. She quickened her pace and began to bang on the door.

"Leanne! Open the door! What's wrong?"

The blood was pounding so loudly in Raitt's ears that he barely heard Leanne Kent's screams, or the pounding on the door. Neither did he feel Leanne's fists pounding his back. He was lost in the sensations of his cock buried inside her. She was so wet, her belly so flat . . . He leaned his head down so that he could bite her hard little tits, tits that were nothing like Rae's milk-filled udders.

Rae . . .

Suddenly, the face of his wife invaded his mind . . . his wife, who he hadn't thought of for hours . . .

"Leanne!" he heard a woman's voice call, and damned if it didn't *sound* like Rae.

"Rae —" Leanne started to call, but Raitt stopped her. She began to writhe beneath him with renewed strength,

246

threatening to slide from under him. He fought her, and finally slapped her, stunning her for a moment. He stood up and retrieved his knife from the floor, where it had fallen when he dropped his pants. With his pants still around his ankles, he leaned over and cleanly cut Leanne Kent's throat. Her blood spurted up, slashing him on the chest, and then the cabin door opened and Rae Raitt was standing there . . .

Rae stood in the open doorway and gasped in horror at what she saw.

Leanne Kent was on the bed, her blood still spurting from her slit throat. At the foot of the bed stood a man, covered in blood, his pants down around his ankles.

When Rae realized who the man was, she screamed.

CHAPTER THIRTY-ONE

"Rae," Bert Raitt said, "wait . . ."

"Oh my God," Rae cried out.

She turned and ran.

"Rae," Raitt shouted again, "wait . . ."

He reached down and pulled up his pants. With his knife in his hand, he ran out the door after her.

He neglected to pick up his pistol, which was still on the floor.

Pike was walking through the woods toward the Raitt house when he heard the woman shouting.

He turned and started in that direction. Before long he could hear someone running through the brush, and moments afterward he saw her.

It was Rae Raitt. The pregnant woman came crashing through undergrowth, a look of sheer terror on her face. She was shouting over and over again, her voice tinged with disbelief as well as horror, "Oh God, oh God . . ."

As he moved to intercept her, he saw the man who was chasing her. He was covered with blood and brandishing a blood-stained knife.

Although his face was splattered with blood, Pike recognized him.

Bert Raitt was chasing his wife through the woods, looking for all the world like he intended to kill her.

Rae Raitt couldn't even think. All she could do was run, as fast and as hard as could, until suddenly the pain knifed through her belly and made her stagger and fall to her knees.

The baby! Oh Jesus, she thought, the baby is coming!

Bert Raitt saw his wife fall, and knew that he had her. When he reached her, he stopped to catch his breath. The whites of his eyes stood out starkly against his blood-stained face and he looked like a madman.

"Bert—" Rae said from the ground. She held one hand out to him, and held her belly with the other. "Bert, please . . . the baby . . ."

Baby? Bert Raitt thought. What the hell was she talking about, baby?

He leaned over her with the knife, knowing only that she had seen him kill Leanne Kent. For that, she had to die . . .

Pike saw Rae Raitt fall, and saw Bert Raitt catch up to her. As Raitt leaned over her with his knife, Pike stopped and raised his rifle. He fired, his ball taking Raitt in the hip.

He didn't want the man dead.

Not just yet.

Rae Raitt's eyes were closed against the pain in her belly. She heard the shot but did not see her husband spin and fall. She just lay there on the ground with both hands holding her belly.

Skins McConnell heard the shot. He stopped and looked around, and when he thought he had the location pinpointed, he started running again.

Pike ran up to Rae Raitt and her husband. He had to check Bert first before he could look at the woman.

He stood over Raitt and kicked his knife away, Raitt, bleeding from the hip, stared up at Pike.

"Who the hell are you?" Raitt demanded.

"Your men are all dead, Raitt," Pike said.

"What do you mean, dead?" Raitt said. "They ain't dead."

"Haywood, Hecox, Murphy and Tilson are dead, because I killed them."

"You? Why?"

"Remember a Crow woman, Raitt?" he said. "Remember raping her, and killing her, and burning her cabin? She was my woman, Raitt. Mine."

"An Indian?"

"An Indian," Pike said.

"Oh, God . . ." Rae Raitt moaned from the ground.

Pike backed away from Raitt, keeping him covered with his pistol, and leaned over the woman.

"Ma'am?"

"Help me, please . . ." she said. "My baby . . ."

"Is the baby coming?" Pike asked.

"Yes . . . yes . . ." Rae said. "Help me . . ."

"Is there a doctor?" Pike asked her. "Is there a doctor I can get you?"

Rae Raitt was beyond answering. She had passed out, and Pike saw a spreading wetness between her legs.

"Raitt," he said. "Your wife's going to die without help. Your wife and your baby."

Raitt said nothing.

"Is there a doctor I can get for her?"

Raitt stared up at Pike, then looked over at his wife.

"Raitt!"

The man looked up at Pike and said, "No doctor, but there's a midwife."

"Who is she?"

"Boyd," Raitt said, "Laura Boyd."

Pike heard someone coming up behind him. He turned and saw it was Skins McConnell.

"Pike?"

"Get some help, Skins," Pike said. "She's going to have her baby. Get some men, and a woman named Laura Boyd."

"Pike—"

"Hurry!"

McConnell nodded, turned and ran toward Pierre's Hole. His breath hissed between his teeth as he gritted his teeth against the pain.

Pike looked at Rae again, but she was lying still. He hoped she wasn't already dead.

"What the hell were you thinking?" Pike asked Raitt. "What kind of an animal are you? You not only were about to kill a pregnant woman, but she's your wife! The baby is your child!"

Raitt laid back, putting his head on the ground.

"You wouldn't understand."

"No," Pike said, "you're right, I wouldn't."

He pointed his pistol at Bert Raitt while Raitt was staring at the sky, and pulled the trigger.

EPILOGUE

The death toll in Pierre's Hole was light, all considered. Three merchants had been killed, and one citizen, a woman who had walked into the trading post at the wrong time.

Leanne and Jesse Kent had been killed by Bert Raitt.

Kincaid, Newman and Peters had all been killed by the citizens of Pierre's Hole.

Dan Tilson's death didn't count. It had happened before the fact, and had nothing to do with the attempted robbery of Pierre's Hole.

Bert Raitt had been killed by Pike.

Buck ended up with a bad headache, but no permanent damage.

Laura Boyd not only delivered Rae Raitt's baby, but she also taped Skins McConnell's ribs for him.

But the death that most affected Pike was April Dancer's.

She was the woman killed in the trading post.

It was several days before McConnell was ready to

ride. The night before they were to leave Pierre's Hole they sat at the fire while Buck slept.

"What are you going to do about the boy?" Pike asked.

"Take him with us, I guess," McConnell said. "Somewhere along the line maybe I'll find a good home for him."

"I hope so . . ."

Later McConnell said, "They're calling you the hero of Pierre's Hole, you know."

Pike smiled at his friend and said, "You and I know I'm no hero, don't we?"

Still later . . .

"How's Raitt's wife and son doing?" Pike asked.

"Laura Boyd says they're doing fine," McConnell said.

"She's a good-looking woman," Pike said, "Laura Boyd, I mean."

"I know," McConnell said. "I ain't blind."

"She still retaping your ribs every day?"

"Sure."

"They don't need to be retaped every day, you know."

"I know it," McConnell said, "and you know it . . . but her husband doesn't."

"Sometimes you're a snake, Skins."

McConnell smiled and said, "I know it . . ."

The next morning they saddled their horses, which they had retrieved the night before. Pike didn't want to go into Pierre's Hole again.

"Where to?" McConnell asked.

"Might as well head for Clark's Fork," Pike said. "Just to have a destination."

"How are you doing?"

Pike looked over at his friend and said, "There was a heat inside me that's gone now. Now all I feel is . . . tired."

"You look the same," McConnell said. "I mean, the same as you did before . . ."

"I'm not the same, though," Pike said, "am I, Skins?"

McConnell hesitated a moment, then said, "No, Pike, I reckon you ain't."